Praise for *Straw Dogs*

'A most exciting story . . . the author seems to have an insight into the thought processes of fighting men and can usually manage to turn the screw of anxiety when one had thought there was no play left in it'

Sunday Telegraph

'Williams sets up his drama with gripping skill . . . tremendously well told, with a fierce pace . . . it is in his descriptions of the enclosed village life and in the construction of the tension that Williams is quite exceptional'

Sunday Times

'The story has real pace and excitement'

New Statesman

'One of the best domestic thrillers I've ever read'

Glasgow Herald

'The atmosphere and tension build up to a frightening and well-sustained climax'

Financial Times

'The story is told with a power and a force that fairly sweeps one along'

Evening Standard

Straw Dogs

Formerly: The Siege of Trencher's Farm

Gordon Williams

Bloomsbury Film Classics
The Original Novel

First published 1969 by Secker and Warburg, Great Britain
This paperback edition published 2003

Copyright © 1969 by Gordon Williams
Original title: *The Siege of Trencher's Farm*

The moral right of the author has been asserted

Bloomsbury Publishing plc, 38 Soho Square, London W1D 3HB

A CIP catalogue is available from the British Library

ISBN 0 7475 6603 8

10 9 8 7 6 5 4 3 2 1

All papers used by Bloomsbury Publishing are natural,
recyclable products made from wood grown in sustainable,
well-managed forests. The manufacturing processes
conform to the environmental regulations of the
country of origin.

Printed in Great Britain by Clays Ltd, St Ives, plc

CHAPTER ONE

In the same year that Man first flew to the Moon and the last American soldier left Vietnam there were still corners of England where lived men and women who had never travelled more than fifteen miles from their own homes. They had spent all their lives on the same land that had supported their fathers and grandfathers and great-grandfathers and unknown generations before that.

The neighbouring parishes of Dando and Compton Wakley formed such a place. Here, in the same generation that produced men who looked back at Earth from the blackness of outer space, existed Englishmen to whom the two hundred mile journey to London was an almost legendary experience, something that might happen once in a lifetime, if at all.

Progress had brought only superficial change to the life of Dando. Farmhouses built three and four hundred years ago, when walls were made by trampling mud and straw, now bore television aerials on their chimneys. Horses had given way to tractors. The narrow roads of the parishes, their banks so high they were little better than tunnels with an open roof, now had metalled surfaces and at night the jinking lantern on the shaft of a wooden cart had been replaced by the low-angled searchlight sweep of motor-car headlamps. The children of the district no longer had to walk six or seven miles to and from the primary school at Compton Wakley; instead they were collected in the morning by a single-decker bus paid for by the County Education Committee and brought back home in the evening.

Ancient inns to which farming men, generations of them, had walked three and four miles in the dark, after twelve hours toil in the fields, now sold mass-produced beer brought by lorries from the cities.

Yet these changes were akin to the crippled wing which a hen plover drags over grass when man or beast approaches her nest. They were a disguise behind which the old ways and the old ideas lived on as before.

The face of the short, squat man with the black hair on the

7

tractor seat was identical to the face of the man who had worked the same ground a thousand years ago.

At dusk on an autumn evening when the sky was a deep blue canvas smeared by fingers of flame cast by a burning sun, when haunting mists crept down from the dark hills of the moor, it was possible to stand by a wooden gate and look over fields and hedges and woods and see a farmhouse light winking across a shadowy valley and to think ... of the men who had lived here before, of rough-clad armies coming over the bare brows of those same hills, of the savage fair-haired men who came from the sea, of kings and nobles on panoplied horses....

Also at night, in the dim light thrown by a single, cobwebby electric bulb over the encrusted walls of a barn corner, it was possible to stand on a hard earth floor and drink cold, bitter cider drawn from mighty black barrels made by long-dead coopers who had talked among themselves of Napoleon Bonaparte. The tongues of the men who drank the cider were as strange to the outside ear as the dialects of foreign jungles. The names of the men were names that were written in the Conqueror's Domesday Book, the same names that had lived on the same farms since Drake sailed from Plymouth to smash the might of Spain.

Some of these men, it is true, had gone away from Dando to fight in the last war, the modern war. They had fought in African deserts and Burmese jungles and Italian mud. Yet, unlike the city men, they had come home determined to maintain the old ways, as though the modern civilisation they had seen was an alien land from which they had escaped. Some of these men who drank cider in the year of the moon rockets could not read or write. Some, if a stranger were present, could adopt the speech of the cities. Some could not.

And some who could, would not. For there was a dark side to this corner of England. Cut off from the rest of that side of the country by low hills and served by roads no wider than a single motor car, the farmers and villagers had over the years come to regard themselves more and more as being apart from other people. Geography was one reason for the isolation of the two parishes. Poverty was another. The land here was poor. The men, whether they owned the land or worked for someone else, had to spend long, dreary days in the fields. Few of them could afford to go away to seaside towns for holidays – and

8

neither did outsiders come to Dando, for it was not a city man's idea of beautiful countryside. To the south and west lay the Moor. It, they said, had a climate all its own, a meeting point for cold rain-winds from the Atlantic Ocean. On the edge of the Moor, standing as it were between Dando and the sun, was the great bulk of Torn Hill. Even in summer Torn seemed to cast a shadow over the two parishes, robbing them of warmth.

So the outside world tended to pass Dando by. And Dando people, either from pride or fear – if the two are divisible – preferred to stay within the boundaries of their own parishes, to be born there, raised there, wed there, and buried there. It was said that some of the older people, especially the women, could give a family connection between almost any two individuals in the area.

Dando marries its own, was a local saying. In neighbouring towns this was often accompanied by knowing looks and the shaking of heads. Dando, they said, had married its own for too many years. And no closed family could be without its dark secrets. The few outsiders who did buy land within the boundaries of the two parishes might spend a lifetime without hearing these secrets, for some things could not be told to strangers and a stranger could be any man whose father had not been born in the parish.

The outsider might hear hinted references to things he did not understand. He might ask, for instance, why a certain pasture behind the woods which stood above the village of Dando Monachorum was called Soldier's Field. He would be told that ancient history had it that a soldier was once murdered there. He would not be told that there was one old man still in the village who had been in the field the night the soldier's head was hacked from his body by a hedge-cutter's billhook. He would not be told that there were men and women who could remember their fathers being out that night, when the soldier came from the barracks at Plymouth and met twelve-year-old Mary Tremaine on the road from the ford at Fourways Cross ... and how the men came from farmhouses and cottages and the Dando Inn when the soldier – a deserter, a man of some strength who had crossed the Moor on foot – was caught. Only the men who were there could tell what was in their minds as they slew the soldier, each man taking his turn with the billhook so that all would have taken part.

9

The men of Dando, as the area of the two parishes was usually known, had been apart for a thousand years and more and when the outside world threatened them and their land they knew best the strength of their own apartness. A family had to guard its own secrets. . . .

CHAPTER TWO

That morning George Magruder pulled back the red velvet curtains of the upstairs bedroom window to see the English countryside under snow for the first time. A foot or more had fallen during the night and apart from the black lines of the hedges and a few isolated trees everything was white from the little garden wall in front of the house right to the top of Torn Hill, whose great breast shape stood starkly bright against the darker grey of the sky. It was a cold, bleak scene. Nothing moved out there. He broke an icicle off the roof overhang, kneeling on the wide window ledge to reach out, his pyjama-clad arm feeling the biting cold of the east wind.

He walked on bare feet across bare, polished boards to the bed where his wife, Louise, was still asleep. With his left hand he smoothed a few strands of long, dark hair from her face. As usual she slept with her mouth open, a habit he had failed to cure.

On impulse he laid the icicle gently between her lips and bent over to kiss her cheek. She came out of sleep slowly at first, until her teeth and lips closed on the cold sliver of ice.

"What's that? Get it away!" she grimaced, her face contorted in apparently real horror.

"Look," he said, holding it up before her eyes. "It's only an icicle."

"Is it meant to be funny or something?" She turned on to her back, her face away from him. "I was having such a lovely dream, too."

"We've had snow during the night. England looks distinctly Siberian."

She showed no enthusiasm when he told her to get up and see the snow. He went to the window.

"It's different from all those Christmas cards," he said. "I can't see any holly. Where's the red-cheeked coachman and the robin redbreast?"

"I hope the bloody road isn't blocked," she said, yawning. "This is the last day the butcher calls before the holiday."

"We might be snowed in for days and days. Wouldn't that be romantic?"

"Not if we have to eat tins of catfood."

"You going to get Karen up? She'll love it."

"I suppose so. That's about all you can say for it, children like it."

He threw the icicle out of the window and went to the bathroom, which opened off the small, square landing at the end of the upstairs corridor. Karen was never at her best in the mornings, he told himself. He began to hum. The wind had blown snow in drifts against the right-angled wall of the old stable and garage, two buildings which, with the house, formed three sides of a square. The fourth side was the beginning of a long, narrow lawn which ran between high banks to a point wedged at the meeting of their own track road and one of the Knapman fields.

As usual he shaved, although it was unlikely he would leave the house that day. It helped to freshen him up for the day's work at his desk in the downstairs study. Sometimes he made a joke of this to Louise, saying that shaving was his equivalent of the Englishman dressing for dinner in the heart of the jungle. Since they'd come to live in Trencher's Farm she had not been receiving these silly little jokes of his with her usual tolerance. Lately he'd been trying consciously to bring a little more astringency into what he liked to describe as 'the furniture of their connubial conversation'. The icicle, he thought, had been a mistake.

George and Louise Magruder had been married for nine years. For most of that time they had lived near Philadelphia in the United States, where he was a senior member of the English Department at the University of Philadelphia. They had met at the home of the Wilshires, Maurice Wilshire having married Louise's sister, whom he'd met at Cambridge. This sabbatical year had seemed an excellent opportunity to combine two ambitions: her desire to take him to England to show him *her* country and his need to find a quiet place where he could write the final draft of his definitive study on Branksheer, the late eighteenth-century English diarist. Of course

11

Branksheer was now part of the common transatlantic heritage and most of the useful papers were safe and secure in America, but it had seemed appropriate that the final version should be written in England. He had been hoping, perhaps childishly, that some of the atmosphere might rub off on him. He felt he knew everything there was to know about Branksheer without understanding a single thing about the man.

They had advertised in *The Times* (of London) for a suitable house in the West Country and it was Louise who had plumped for Trencher's Farm. A farm in name only, the land having been sold off many years ago, the house was a long, white-walled building with a study, sitting-room, dining-room and kitchen on the ground floor, and four bedrooms, bathroom and lavatory upstairs.

The general effect was of a squat, immensely sturdy building designed to stand up to the worst winds and snow the Moor could hurl down on the two parishes. The clay and straw walls – a method of construction known as 'cob' – were two feet thick. In the main part of the house, which was said to date back four hundred years, the windows were little more than three feet square, as though the original builders begrudged every inch that didn't give the inhabitants massive protection. Giant, smoke-blackened oak beams traversed the ceilings of the downstairs rooms. At the rear the kitchen and the upstairs bathroom formed an extension built on since the war, its walls of brick and its windows more in accordance with modern ideas. When they were inspecting the house George had pointed out several diagonal cracks on the matt white walls of the downstairs rooms, but the estate agent had laughed and said those cracks had probably been there since the days of Cromwell.

They had taken a six months lease in the first instance at what Louise said was a fairly steep rent of twelve guineas a week. He had converted this into dollars per month (as rent was calculated in America) and found it remarkably cheap. However, having been married so long to an Englishwoman he was well aware of the reputation Americans had for money consciousness and he took care, when speaking to English people, not to boast about the deal.

When he had shaved, his cheeks and chin tingling with Old Spice, he went back to the bedroom and dressed in his fawn Levis and red tartan shirt. For a man who was thirty-five and did nothing more strenuous than walk and swim he thought he was in pretty fair shape.

"It's my morning walk that does it," he said to Louise, who was still in bed. She seemed bored. "I know you think I'm silly, my routines and all, but it isn't as silly as you think. If I didn't have a routine I couldn't keep in the swing of the work."

"As the monk said to the abbess, you're a creature of habit, George. Who are you keeping in good shape for?"

"Who?"

"What, then? D'you still think they'll maybe ask you to run in the Olympics?"

It was better to leave Louise alone in this mood. For a long time he'd been sure the difference in their nationalities was of no significance, but in the three months they'd been living here at Trencher's Farm she'd changed, somehow. Had she ever felt like a stranger in the States? He was sure she goddam well had not, but he certainly was beginning to feel like a stranger here in England, here in his own home.

When they'd first arrived, he'd gone walking, to establish some kind of orientation. The obvious way was to turn right at the junction of their track and the "real" road, which was, admittedly, metalled but so narrow that when cars met one had to back up to a field gate or to one of the shallow indentations cut into the high banking. Having turned right, the road went downhill for about two miles, the longest two miles he had ever walked in his life, until it wandered into the village of Dando Monachorum. The name, he thought, was ridiculously at odds with the look of the place, which was not one of those thatched villages they used for British ads in tho *New Yorker*. The name was the *only* picturesque thing about it.

Louise had said she wanted to find a house 'off the beaten track', away from the 'touristy' parts. By Heaven, she'd achieved her wish. Any tourists who came to Dando Monachorum had to be nuts. There were seven or eight shabby cottages with low roofs, some thatched and some corrugated. There was a red-brick Methodist chapel, an ill-favoured building which, for some reason, seemed to have been built in such a way that all sides of it were always on the wrong side for the sun. There was a grey-stone school no longer functioning as a school and used for bingo on Monday nights and occasional village functions. And there was the pub, the Dando Inn.

Louise had said the locals would take some time getting used

13

to them, but he had seen no reason for encouraging mutual suspicion and one night he'd walked down to the Inn hoping to strike up some kind of thing with these fearsome villagers. The bar was smaller than their sitting-room. It contained seven or eight men and youths who seemed to do little drinking but a lot of dart-playing. He'd felt like a complete stranger who had walked uninvited into someone's family home. The men stared at him and then turned their eyes away when he stared back and said good evening.

At the bar, a small counter hardly longer than his desk, he asked for a small beer. The landlord seemed pleasant enough, although it did strike George Magruder that the man showed very little curiosity. After all, how many Americans did they get in a joint like this? While most of the men looked like farmworkers or auto-mechanics, the landlord had a faint air of having come down in the world. He wore a shirt and tie and the jacket of a blue suit.

He tried casual conversation about the weather and the beer, but the landlord made only non-committal replies, the kind that leave no conversational bridges. If he'd been in a similar situation at home (unlikely, he thought) he might have asked the man to give everyone a drink on him, but Louise had warned him against such typically unwelcome American habits. She said these kind of country folk would only respect you if you were as close with money as they were themselves. What the hell, he wasn't interested in respect, only in getting somebody to talk to, but the customers ignored him for their interminable darts and the landlord offered not one word that could be construed as conversation.

"What was it like, darling?" Louise asked when he got home.

"I was hardly overwhelmed by traditional English hospitality, if that's what you mean," he said. "Going by tonight we'll have to learn to make our own conversation."

Louise had been slightly worried all the time he'd been gone. She knew more about the kind of people who lived in a place like this than George could ever hope to. To them a Londoner was a foreigner – an American might as well be from outer space. Yet she'd often been surprised by George's American ability to crash into situations which she found delicate – and to come out on top. It was one of the things she had admired him for.

After that night George Magruder began to wonder con-

14

stantly if a man *could* exist purely within the society of his own family. Much as he loved Louise they had been married for nine years and the time for mutual exploration by conversation (or anything else) was past. And there was a limit to the satisfaction one could obtain from the company of an eight-year-old girl.

It seemed likely that for at least six months Trencher's Farm would be his only world. Well, countless men had lived like this in the frontier days. A man and his wife alone in a brutal, unknown world, living on their own resources. A man who'd come to a virgin valley and carved out a piece of land and fought off Indians and survived drought and ploughed and reaped and lived through hunger and blizzards and ... it was the kind of childish thought, Louise said, that prevented him from turning completely into a stuffy old academic with his nose buried in the late eighteenth century.

That same evening, after he'd left the bar, the men had talked about him. They, of course, knew who he was, the rich yank who'd rented Trencher's, some kind of professor. The ones who had been in the army didn't like Americans for they knew that Americans were loudmouths with fat bellies and a yellow streak down their backs a yard wide. This view had come to be accepted by those who hadn't been in the army.

Tom Hedden, a Dando farmer, had been throwing for double sixteen to win the game when George Magruder left. Normally he could throw three darts into the treble bed ten times out of ten, but his concentration had been broken.

"They'm yanks be takin' over the whole world," he said, pulling out his darts with an open petulance often found among simple, masculine men. "How does 'ee afford Trencher's then, what they'm say the rent be, Norman?"

"Twelve guinea a week, I hear. More'n some folk get for feedin' whole family."

"He seemed a nice enough bloke," said Harry Ware, the landlord. The men made a joke of this landlord's impartiality.

"Oh aye, 'ee's a friend o' yourn so long he'm not short o' a bob or two."

Harry Ware had grown used to the sarcasm and the jeers and the insults which formed most of the conversation of his customers. They were people who liked nothing better than to put something 'over' on somebody else, friend or foe didn't matter. Harry Ware had bought the Dando Inn *because* it was

15

so small and so far out of the way of crowds. He and his wife had thought it would give them a nice easy living after several years in a busy place on a main road not far from Torquay. He had been a grocer in Sunderland, where he was born, before going into the licensed trade. Although he had lived in the West Country for more than twenty years he didn't really understand the people. In this he showed greater intelligence than many allegedly cleverer men, for he knew he didn't understand them. If you came from anywhere else in England, these thick-necked, round-faced West Countrymen were regarded almost as clowns; they had a reputation for being the most obsequious and servile and obedient soldiers in the nation. They would touch their forelocks or salute an officer and take the most ridiculous order without question when a Geordie or a Taff or a Scouse or a Jock would argue – or fight.

Yet beneath this stolid, almost bovine exterior, he knew there were dark twists in their minds. A Glasgow Jock was quick with his fists but these men were different, they could go for years without showing emotion and then ... their blood was said to be very old, going back to ancient days. He was always very careful. These men were his regulars and he more or less lived off what they spent every night. On Saturdays and Sundays other farmers and villagers increased his takings, but without the men in the bar that night he could not make his week's wages.

Tom Hedden had a small farm, only fifty-one acres which he worked alone with the help of his fifteen-year-old son, Bobby. Then there was Bertie Scutt, who lived off his wife's ten family allowances and the unemployment pay he drew between intermittent spells of casual work. Chris Cawsey was about twenty-two, he worked as a mechanic as the Compton Wakley garage; Harry Ware thought there was something almost girlish about Chris Cawsey even though he owned a motor-bike and wore big leather belts with fancy buckles.

Phillip Riddaway was the biggest man present, a thick lump of a farm-worker with a big round red face and hands like a bunch of bananas. Phillip worked for Colonel Scott at the Manor Farm. Everybody knew he was thick in more ways than one. Sometimes Chris Cawsey and Norman Scutt – Bertie's son – would tease him to a point where an ordinary man would have lost his temper, but Phillip never did. The more they laughed at him the more he seemed to like them.

16

Bert Voizey was a carpenter and, it was said, an expert poacher. An insignificant looking man, he had a reputation for being able to snare foxes with wire and whenever a local farmer was infested with rats he would be called in to clear them for a flat price of two pounds. He had some recipe of his own for poison.

Norman Scutt was Bertie's oldest son, although in the bar they spoke to each other like mates rather than father and son. Harry Ware didn't like Norman, who wore his hair in some new fancy style with long black sideboards. For one thing Norman fairly often got drunk (something the other men rarely did, it being a matter of pride not to show it), but apart from that, he had a record. His last sentence had been nine months for burglary and before that he'd been in court for various offences, some of violence and some purely larcenous.

When closing time came it was generally Norman Scutt who wanted to go on drinking and while, like any other landlord of an out-of-the-way pub, Harry Ware was willing to stretch the law by half an hour or so to keep the goodwill of his regulars, he always had a slight fear of Norman turning nasty.

"I don't get twelve in my wages, do I?" said Phillip Riddaway, who took his time about entering conversations.

"That's because you'm thick, Phil," said Norman. "Them yanks aint thick, they'm richer'n you nor I'll ever be. You see his wife, then? Cor, Phil, she'd give you a good time, you dirty big booger."

Phil grinned. Norman was always telling him about women. Phil had never done anything to a woman. Norman was always saying he'd have to try it before he reached forty or it would be too late. Phil liked hearing Norman talk about women. Norman had done it with lots of women.

"Aye, it's all right for them yanks, bein' rich like," said Tom Hedden. "Us got to scratch for the price of a pint'r two."

Harry Ware wondered if Norman, who had not been out of Exeter gaol for two months, might be thinking of doing a bit of burglary up at Trencher's. The others always said in Norman's favour that he'd never stolen from anybody in Dando, but a Yank wasn't local. . . .

When he went downstairs it was George Magruder's routine to pick up the morning's post from behind the front door and

17

then to rake out and fill the two fires. In the sitting-room there was an *Esse*, a glass-fronted slow burner which heated water for six radiators throughout the house. Every morning when he raked out the night's ash he told himself how lucky they'd been to find an English house with central heating.

Having made a parcel of the *Esse* ash, using *The Times Business Section* as a wrapper, he then went through the sitting-room and the dining-room to the kitchen, having to duck his head to avoid the low oak beam above the dining-room door. In the kitchen he cleaned out the *Aga*, which the estate agents had called the Rolls-Royce of cookers. On its two hot plates, normally capped by massive stainless steel lids on hinges, Louise did all their cooking, and the slow-burning fire also provided hot water for the kitchen and bathroom. Although he knew the *Aga* was of modern and scientific design he liked to think it was the kind of stove women cooked on when men were out ploughing virgin prairies or branding longhorn calves. It was the first time in his life he had seen anything seriously cooked by other means than electricity. It gave life a kind of barbecue flavour.

He went out of the kitchen door into the porch, carrying the *Aga* rakings in its ash-shovel; he put down both lots of ash to pull on his rubber boots. These had tractor type soles and had been left behind in the coal-shed by a previous tenant. He had bought special felt sole-linings but even with those he still thought there was something unhygienic about wearing another person's castoffs. If it had not been for certain ridicule by Louise – who tended to laugh at his awareness of germs – he would have burned them and bought himself a new pair. He felt this sort of detail might possibly help towards creating the right mental attitude for writing the Branksheer book. Squire and scholar and diarist as he was, Branksheer had lived in what could only be described as squalor. George Magruder just could not tune in on the wavelength of a man who was at home in Latin and Greek and corresponded with Europe's leading classicists, and at the same time took head-lice for granted and the pox as almost inevitable. He and Louise often argued whether it was sophisticated to desire clinical sterility. She took the view that the truly mature man would not have a complex about dirt.

He opened the porch door and walked through a foot of snow towards the corner of the house, passing the kitchen window. Between the corner of the garage and the house there was a heavy wooden partition into which was set a door. He slid back the bolt and backed through, both hands occupied with ash. He let the wooden door slam behind him. He walked along the end wall of the house to the corner, where the frozen surface of the snow now glinted in the bright December sun.

In front of the house there was a small paved forecourt in which a few rose-bushes and shrubs grew in beds cut out of the paving stones. These were protected by a low brick wall which ran the length of the house front. With six inches of snow on top of the wall, it looked like a slice of Christmas cake topped by sugar icing.

Previous tenants had dumped their ashes in untidy heaps across the road behind an old shed, but he had seen a more useful and tidier way of disposing of them. Every morning he brought the two lots out to the front of the house and put them in pot-holes in the track road. Already he had levelled up most of the larger holes in front of the house. The distance between the house and the real road was about four hundred yards. He had a curious little ambition – to see their track completely smoothed off by waste from the two fires. Occasionally he would try to work out how long it would take. The answer varied from three to five years. But it was a useful task to launch and he could only hope future tenants would carry on the good work.

That morning he could not see the pot-holes for snow and after some thought he dumped the contents of the parcel and the shovel roughly opposite the garage door. When the snow melted he could sweep the ash into the nearest hole. Only then did he think of looking at the scenery. As usual he was offended by the rickety old shed across the road. There was something slovenly about people who would spend a lot of money putting in new heating and electric wiring and modern bathroom fittings – and then leave a tumbledown shack like that right smack in line with the house's front windows.

He was learning a lot about the English. For one thing they were not the cosy little islanders they were pictured in the States. Of course there *were* odd characters around who looked as though they'd come straight from a Peter Sellers film, but for every tweedy old gent like Colonel Scott there were others; old women who muttered as they moved silently about the dark gardens of the village cottages; the dark-haired,

19

unsmiling man who walked the road secretively, as though making for some age-old pagan rite under an oak tree.

One of the impressions he had gathered was of an unsuspected brutality. When he looked at the cold slopes of Torn Hill he thought of the big, prison-like building which stood beyond it; Two Waters they called it, officially described as Two Waters Institution for the Criminally Insane, a grim stone fortress rising out of the bleak slopes of the moor. He could never believe that a people who had split the atom and produced Robert Graves could be primitive enough to put their mentally sick in a place like Two Waters. Quite apart from the fact that no building erected during the reign of Queen Victoria could possibly be suitable for the treatment of extreme forms of mental illness, it wasn't reassuring to think of murderers and perverts of all kinds only ten or so miles away. There wasn't even a wall round the place, only high barbed-wire fencing. And that had only been erected out of public indignation after an infamous escape.

The English, he often thought, could yield to no people in their ability to accept various manifestations of unconscious barbarity....

Louise Magruder (*née* Hartley) watched her husband from the upstairs bedroom window. An attractive woman of thirty-five, she was doing her hair in the currently fashionable Jane Austen cut, severe lines over the ears and a bun at the back. She thought she would wear the white blouse with the frilly front and leg-of-mutton sleeves. Perhaps she was a little too *mature* to be dressing up like a teenage girl but stuck here in the wilds of nowhere there was little else to provide amusement. It didn't help her general state of irritation to know she had been largely responsible for bringing them to live at Trencher's Farm.

"Karen, aren't you up yet?" she called into the wardrobe-cupboard set into the wall of their bedroom. On the other side of the wall was Karen's wardrobe, both cut into the clay and straw wall. Voices carried clearly through the thin wood that separated the two cupboards.

"Coming, Mummy."

Knees slightly splayed, as though that would bring her hair nearer her twisted arms, she put a pin into the bun at the back of her neck. George had dumped his ash on the snow. She knew she was being unfair but there was something essentially

20

silly about him. The shape of his head, for instance. He insisted on having his hair cut short although she told him his large, pointed ears should be made less obvious. In Philadelphia, where she had been the foreigner, she had never thought of him as anything but a normal husband; now that they'd been living in England for three months she could see things about him, *American* things.

It wasn't just that he made a great fuss about making ice when they had people in for drinks and it wasn't just that he couldn't make a simple telephone call without remarking on the *dreadful* British phone system. She was used to ice in her drinks and she wasn't the hysterical patriotic type who had to defend the indefensible – American telephones made English ones seem like something out of the Middle Ages, if that wasn't an anachronism or something. Anyway, she knew what she meant.

No, it was his mind she could now see as being different. In America she'd almost forgotten what Englishmen were like but since she'd come back she'd found herself continually comparing George to other men, Colonel Scott, for instance, and Gregory Allsopp the doctor. In some ways George was more mature than them – he could hold his liquor better for a start, not like Colonel Scott who, judging by the colour of his face, should have had enough practice. Yet there was something infantile about the seriousness with which he took things like drinking. He hated anything facetious and when he fell into the trap of taking their little jokey remarks seriously he tended to sulk when he realised they had not been serious.

Driving was another of his weak spots. He was a good driver and he saw no reason for saying otherwise. Gregory Allsopp was probably just as good but like most intelligent Englishmen she'd ever known he continually made himself out to be a blundering buffoon who'd only escaped serious accidents by a lifetime of phenomenal luck. George didn't like that kind of affectation.

He took the *stupidest* things seriously. Like his weight. If he went over his hundred and fifty pounds by so much as one pound he would first complain about the undependability of British bathroom scales, then he'd cut down on potatoes and bread and *everything*. He didn't smoke – of course. Impeccable, that was it about Americans, they had a neurotic fixation on health and hygiene.

She thought of the one lover she'd had since their marriage. Patrick had bad breath and a severe case of body odour and was even given to farting in public. She giggled into the mirror. She could imagine the hilarious look on George's face if someone farted out loud at dinner. The more she thought about it the more she laughed to herself.

"I'm up, Mother," said Karen. Not for the first time since she'd come back to England, Louise Magruder had to remind herself that her daughter was not pretending to be an American. She *was* an American. . . .

Louise was pouring cold milk on their breakfast cereal when Karen said the cat's saucer had not been touched during the night. The cat, a half-grown tom they'd acquired from the Knapmans, had not come back from its evening run the night before and they'd left its saucer of tinned meat in the coal shed.

"I wouldn't worry, he probably got caught in the snow, he'll be holed up somewhere snug and sound, cats can take care of themselves," said Louise.

"Cats don't like snow," said Karen. "To a cat snow is a drag. Cats are very fastidious, Mother."

"I know, dear. That's why they always come home, they can't *stand* other people's houses." Like George, she thought.

Her husband came into the porch, where he carefully removed his rubber boots and put on leather moccasins before stepping on to the kitchen linoleum.

"It's a funny old country this," he said. "Karen, you've never seen real *English* snow. It's peculiar, you know that? It's *warm*."

"Snow isn't warm, Daddy."

Louise remembered when Karen had insisted on calling him Pop. It had taken time to cure her of *that*.

"English snow is warm. Isn't that right, Mother?"

She didn't really know why she felt so irritated.

After breakfast they went outside to throw snowballs. Louise felt confused. Karen was far too dignified for a child of her age. She wouldn't run and yell like a normal child, at least like normal children Louise remembered from her childhood. On the other hand George's antics seemed forced and unnatural, as though he didn't really understand why people threw snowballs but was willing to imitate the actions. Rather like his jokes.

Louise determined to suppress this recent tendency to criticise her husband and daughter. She allowed Karen to hit her with a snowball and then ran, screaming, through the door by the garage. They were standing in the snow on the road when George let out a horrified yell. He stood still, his face transfixed in horror, looking down.

"What's wrong, dear?" Louise cried. "Did nasty snow go down your boots, you poor old thing?"

He didn't answer.

She thought he might be having a game, tricking her into coming near so that he could rub snow down her neck, but he wasn't that good an actor.

"I stood on *something*," he said.

"It's all that ash," she said, smiling.

"No, it was soft. I felt it."

She went across and poked the toe of her Wellington boot into the hard snow where he had been standing. There was something there. She scraped at the snow with her instep. Karen threw a snowball which spattered on George's tartan shirt. He didn't seem to notice.

Her toe uncovered something brown. She scraped some more. She uncovered a piece of tabby fur and then a leg.

"It's the cat," she said. "It's dead."

"Our cat? Is it our cat, Mother?"

"Yes, I'm afraid so. Lift it up, George, I wonder what killed it."

"Lift it? I don't want to touch it! *You* lift it."

It didn't seem important. She scraped away the rest of the snow round the cat's body. It was lying fully stretched on its side. She bent down and picked it up, her finger and thumb holding the very tip of its tail. It's head swung round gently, the whiskers dusty with snow. Something hung from its neck. It was a piece of thin rope, the tail end of a noose which had been pulled tightly into its neck.

"It's been strangled," she said angrily.

"Maybe it got caught in a trap," said George, who had backed away a step or two.

"They use wire for snares, not rope. Look, there's a knot in the rope. Somebody did this deliberately."

"Kids, probably," said George.

"Oh, Daddy, I don't want to look at it," said Karen. Not tearfully, as Louise remembered herself when her dog, Billy,

23

had been run over by a car when she was young.

"Yeah, get rid of it," said George. He looked at his wrist-watch. "I'm going in to start work. Toss it behind the old shed, we can bury it later."

Louise carried the dead cat to the dump behind the shed. She dropped it on the snow-covered mound of papers and other rubbish which they burned once a week. She hoped they would be able to bury it or burn it before it began to smell.

When she came round the shed both Karen and George had gone inside. She thought of winter days when her father went out with nets and guns and ferrets and came home carrying dead rabbits with blood on their soft grey fur. She'd often stood beside the sink and watched him skin and gut the rabbits. . . .

Once a week Niles had to be taken to the county hospital for his kidney injections. That day there were no other patients for the ambulance run and Senior Male Nurse Frank Pawson thought the trip might be cancelled because of the snow. However Doctor Tindall said the road had been cleared by a County Council snowplough and Niles must have his injection and check-up.

"Come on, Henry old chappie," said Pawson to Niles. "Time for your weekly jaunt."

"Can I look out of the window?" asked Niles. He always did ask, although he'd been going back and forward to the county hospital for years and was always allowed to look out of the window.

"Sure, Henry, you can look at all the lovely snow. Nature's magic carpet."

When Pawson had first transferred to Two Waters Niles was still a big name and he could remember the male nurses sweating every time they had to take him for a bath or to the clinic. They weren't afraid of Niles, no grown man had ever had reason to fear Henry. They were terrified in case they made some mistake and he escaped again. People had been dismissed the last time Henry had escaped. After the public inquiry into the security system a fence had been put round the grounds even although no inmate was ever allowed beyond the high wall of the exercise garden at the rear. Niles had been put under twenty-four-hour surveillance, not allowed to sleep without a

24

light on in his room, inspected every half hour to make sure the sleeping figure was not a dummy.

As if Henry would ever have had the brains to think of building a dummy. To look at him now you'd never believe this was *the* Henry Niles. He looked like a man of fifty – and he was only thirty-four. He didn't look capable of tying his own shoelaces. A helpless little man. Pawson instinctively took his elbow as he made to climb the steps into the rear of the ambulance.

"Strike a bloody light," said the ambulance driver, who, like Pawson, was originally a Londoner. "I thought I'd get a buckshee day off with this snow. Couldn't he have missed his shot for one bleeding week?"

"Doctor's orders," said Pawson. "How long d'you think it'll take on these roads?"

"Should make good time. Not much traffic about today." The ambulance driver grinned. "In fact, you could say only a madman would be out driving in conditions like this."

Pawson didn't laugh.

Henry Niles sat on the bench, his body twisting round so that he could look through the top three inches of clear glass. It was the only view he'd had of the outside world in nine years. This was the big treat of his week. Only he knew what he thought about as he looked through the glass slit. For ten years he had hardly spoken more than a few sentences at any one time. At his two trials and at the public inquiry into the escape it had been stated by psychiatrists that he had the mental age of a child of eight.

The ambulance pulled away from the main gate of Two Waters Institution for the Criminally Insane and picked up speed on a hard layer of snow left by the ploughs. The driver thought he might do the journey to and from the county hospital in fast time. With only one patient to be treated he stood a good chance of being home by five o'clock.

In the back of the ambulance Pawson brought out a folded copy of the *Daily Mail* from his hip pocket. It was his ambition to complete the crossword. He took no notice of Henry Niles who watched the snowy wastes of the huge moor. Frank Pawson found he couldn't concentrate on the crossword clues. Today, he'd made up his mind, he would *definitely* ask Kate Grady to go out with him. . . .

CHAPTER THREE

It had been the Reverend William Hood's idea to improve the community spirit of Dando Monachorum by organising a children's Christmas party on the Wednesday before Christmas Day, which fell on the Friday. The party was to take place between four-thirty and six-thirty in the school. Then, at seventhirty, there was to be the first dance held in the village for some years.

"That will give them an hour to take the children home and get back," he said to his church warden, Bill Knapman, who was not enthusiastic.

"There's a lot of folk won't come out again," he said. "Who's going to look after the children so's they can go dancing?"

"They've all got somebody who can baby-sit for one night," said the Rev. Hood. "They manage well enough to come to bingo every Monday."

Bill Knapman changed the grounds of his attempt to dissuade the Rev. Hood.

"It's not as though there's a lot of young folks who want to dance," he said. "They all go to Compton Fitzpaine if they want that sort of thing."

"Precisely," said the Rev. Hood. "It's about time we did something for them here in Dando. If we don't make the effort we'll never get *anything* going around here. One would think you didn't want to improve the quality of the community."

"It's not that, Mr. Hood," said Knapman, who was eight years older than the minister. "The people about here aren't very community-minded. They don't like a lot of outsiders comin' in, either, that's why they stopped the Saturday night dances in the first place, we were gettin' all they teenagers and whatnot, drinkin' and makin' trouble."

He had been church warden under four vicars, all of them elderly men in semi-retirement, happy to conduct their two services on a Sunday and carry out a minimum of parish visiting. The Rev. Hood was only the curate but because the vicar, the Rev. Thomas, was ill he'd been in charge of the parish for two months. He had not been ordained long. Much as he supported the church, as a much-needed influence in these unsatisfactory times, Knapman had no great respect for the curate. He told himself that he was only trying to save the man from embarrassment. The dance would doubtless be a flop.

"We *want* some life about the village," said the Rev. Hood. "That's most of the trouble about these rural backwaters, the young people have nothing done for them so they drift away to the towns."

"Aye well, there's young people and young people, if you know what I mean. A lot of them like to travel round the villages and disrupt things, fights and the like. I could name a few of our own who're never happy unless they're making trouble."

"Oh, high spirits, yes! That's the whole point. You've got to give the younger generation a chance to get rid of their high spirits the right way. It's when nothing's provided for them they cause mischief. If you don't mind me saying so, Mr. Knapman, I sometimes get the impression you're rather scornful of your fellow men."

"I wouldn't say that," said Bill Knapman. "It's just that there used to be fights and all sorts at the dances here, the Compton Wakley crowd wanted to fight the Fitzpaine crowd and Dando wanted to fight them both – they'd be back and forth from the Inn and drink more'n they could hold and ... well, dances is often just an excuse."

"We can organise a pass-out system," said the curate, brightly determined to push his plan through. "And I'm sure we have enough able-bodied chaps in the parish to handle any trouble. Dando has to move with the times if it isn't going to shrivel up and die."

In the end Bill Knapman had to agree to the dance. It was true what the young curate had said, he didn't have a very high impression of his neighbours, but he knew more about them than any minister, even the old ones. He'd been born and raised within four miles of Dando Monachorum, on a farm his family had owned since seventeen hundred and forty-three. He had gone away to the war and when he'd come back he understood a lot of things about Dando. He could have told the curate of another night when they'd had a dance in the village, the night they found Mary Tremaine on the Fourways road, the night his father and the other men had gone off quietly to the field above the wood. Although he was part of Dando, he had been away into the world, and he could see the parish

27

as it really was. If he had not been born there and brought up to take it for granted that one day he would take over the farm, he doubted very much if he would have chosen to live in Dando.

In the army, when he told them where he came from, they'd make jokes about inbreeding and incest and such things and he could understand why the outside world would think that about the West Country. Even he tended to turn his back on what happened beyond the parish boundaries. These weren't clearly marked but you could *feel* it, you'd be driving along a narrow road and you *knew* when you'd passed out of Dando and Compton, and you wanted to go back. Back to what you knew. Nobody could deny they were a close lot.

When the first sheep had been found brutally stabbed and its throat cut he'd been one of the few who'd been in favour of reporting it to the police at Compton Wakley, the nearest station. Over the last few months six other sheep had been found slaughtered the same way, throat cut and the belly slashed and stabbed by some maniac.

He had told the police and no good had come of it, for none of the farmers had anything to tell the police except how they'd found sheep killed. He had not been popular for having brought the coppers in, prying and asking questions. Everybody had their own theories about who was responsible; it was lucky for Norman Scutt that he'd been in Exeter gaol when the first three were killed, for with him being a criminal already he would have been the obvious man to suspect.

It was a nasty thing to have in the area, with everybody theorising and suspecting, thinking the worst of their neighbours and at the same time, illogically, feeling guilty at being possible suspects themselves.

That dinner-time, the day of the children's party and the dance, he went down to the Inn with his neighbour, Charlie Venner. It was only two days to Christmas and that made it all right to go to the Inn in the middle of the day. In the bar he saw the Scutts, young Cawsey, Phillip Riddaway and Tom Hedden, plus a few more. As usual Tom Hedden was complaining about something – the price Colonel Scott was asking for hay. Hedden's farm was too small to grow all the stuff he needed for his winter stock, it was too small any way you looked at it for a man with five children, but Hedden hung on year after year, out of obstinacy no doubt.

28

"If I give her up what'll I do then, eh?" he'd say. "I'd have to move to a town and work in a factory or summat, not me I don't. They'm tryin' to push us small men off the land, not I they'm don't."

Bill Knapman, whose two hundred and fifty acres gave him a higher place in the Dando scheme of things than Hedden (and a *much* higher place than the Scutts and their friends), understood why Tom Hedden stuck to his farm, although this didn't mean he had much sympathy for the man. A farmer who was continually on the scrounge for one thing or another was a nuisance. No sense, that was Hedden's trouble, he had four sons all at school and a girl – Janice, who'd been born afflicted – five children to feed from a place that wasn't big enough for a man and his wife.

And there was the money Hedden spent in the Inn. The part of Bill Knapman which had been to war understood why a man with too heavy a load on his back took to drink. The other part of him put it down to stupidity; a man who couldn't take care of himself and his family properly should get out. A factory would be a good place for him.

"The professor been in lately then?" Charlie Venner asked loudly, knowing this would give them all a laugh.

"Who, the last of the big spenders?" said Harry Ware. "No, I've been struggling along without his two halves of bitter, thank you very much."

George Magruder would have been surprised to hear what they said about him. He would have realised that their natural awe of a man who could afford Trencher's Farm – without, as far as they knew, doing any work at all – had made them shy of him. If he had offered them a drink they might not have immediately taken him into their innermost confidences, but they would to some extent have accepted him as a *generous* outsider.

Instead they had taken his shyness for contempt. It was one thing for Colonel Scott to treat them with real contempt, for he was superior – he owned the Manor Farm and he was a colonel and he was rich and for centuries they'd lived with the unquestioned superiority of squires. They'd have held Colonel Scott in contempt if he behaved in any other way.

But a yank was different. He was an intruder. Other people had intruded – like the doctor and the curate – but it was different with them.

At half-past two Harry Ware shouted "Time". He put a dish-towel over the beer taps.

"What's all the noise about?" Norman Scutt demanded, shoving his empty pint glass at Harry Ware. "It's Christmas ain't it, give us another bloody pint."

"Sorry, Norman," said Harry Ware, "I got a long night ahead of me with the dance, I need my kip."

"Give us another pint," said Tom Hedden, who looked fairly well gone considering it was dinner-time.

"No more, sorry," said Harry Ware. "Just drink up please, lads, plenty of time tonight for all you can hold."

Tom Hedden had been enjoying himself, the Christmas spirit, all his good mates, darts and talk, the feeling that things weren't so bad – now they were being turfed out. He felt cheated.

"Oh, go on, Harry," he said, his voice thick. "Just another pint like, aint Christmas every day is it?"

Harry Ware shook his head. He had already intended to let Bill Knapman and Charlie Venner stay behind for a few drinks, they were responsible, steady men and they spent well when they came in. Bill Knapman had known this, and he was irritated when Tom Hedden began pleading.

"Right now, your glasses *please*," Harry called.

"Balls to your glasses please, give we another bloody pint," said Norman Scutt.

"Come on, lads, we don't want to make trouble for old Harry here, do we?" said Bill Knapman. It was one of his failings, he recognized, to act as though he had some kind of authority. Yet he couldn't help thinking of the Scutts and that crowd as riff-raff, he'd been brought up that way and for all his experience in the army he couldn't shake it off.

"There's no trouble," said Tom Hedden, almost pathetic in his desire for another drink. "All we'm want's another pint, it aint a lot to ask for regulars like."

Harry Ware shook his head, already washing up glasses. This annoyed Tom Hedden who reckoned he was entitled to a bit more respect. Nor did he like being talked to by Bill Knapman in that high and mighty voice. He banged his glass down on the bar. The glass cracked.

Harry Ware frowned angrily as he swept away the pieces.

"Sorry about the glass," said Tom, leaning forward with his elbows on the bar. "All we'm want is just one more, that's all."

"I told you *no*."

"I aint niver comin' here again, niver givin' you another bloody penny, Harry Ware you –"

Tom Hedden's anger could find no words. He stretched his hand towards Harry Ware, as though to grab him. Bill Knapman was beside him, waiting for something like this. In the army he'd been a military policeman. He was that kind of man.

"Come on, now, Tom, let's not be silly," he said, taking hold of Hedden's sleeve. Tom Hedden shook his arm, trying to free himself.

"I'm as good as anybody," he shouted. "Leggo my arm, Bill Knapman or I'll –"

There might have been a fight, but Bertie Scutt and Bert Voizey got on either side of Tom Hedden and coaxed him out of the bar. Bill Knapman and Charlie Venner stood their ground while the bar emptied. Bill Knapman didn't care very much whether Hedden and Norman Scutt and the rest knew he and Charlie were having a drink after hours. If they weren't such riff-raff they'd get the same treatment. . . .

Just before lunch Louise and Karen went to look for a holly tree with berries, which were scarce that winter. Louise had already decorated the house with paper bells and a small Christmas tree and a few sprigs of holly cut from the trees at the end of the lawn but, as she said, holly without berries wasn't holly at all.

"Jean Knapman says the birds have eaten all the berries," she said to George, knowing how little he was interested in such trivial things. He tried to show some enthusiasm but she knew his mind was on something else. That was one of their troubles – when he was being trivial she wanted to be serious and *vice versa*.

George Magruder was glad she had not asked him to go on the holly hunt. Louise's brother Jeremy and his wife Sophia and their children were arriving the next morning from London and he knew how little work he would get through during their stay. Not that there was any great panic about finishing the Branksheer book but he liked to hold to his working routine as firmly as possible. It was the only discipline available to him here.

Yet when he sat at his desk he felt too disturbed to concentrate. Why hadn't he been able to lift the dead cat? What kind

31

of man could be *paralysed* by the sight of an animal corpse? He poked about on the wide window ledge among the various piles of typed sheets of research notes on Branksheer (B's Three London Trips ... Lydia's Letters ... B on Farming ... B on the Village). Lying on top of them were some small blank gift cards which Louise had put there for him to fill in. He tried to think of original – and witty – inscriptions. He was not in a Christmas mood.

There had been a time when Louise had made him feel particularly manly, in a way that no girl or woman had done before. Perhaps it was her Englishness – she had a softer voice than most women he knew. She was a good listener, something you didn't find too often among American women, especially intelligent ones. Femininity – that was it. She couldn't even drive a car.

But what kind of pattern was emerging now, after nine years of marriage? Pessimistically he thought they might be proving a classic case of opposites attracting each other only, after marriage, to switch direction. The cat had brought it home to him. He'd made her capable. She'd let him become soft. He'd taught her to drive.

The inference that anybody with brains would have to draw was that subconsciously he wanted her to relieve him of the responsibility of masculinity. The classic American syndrome – which he had always felt so glad that he did not suffer from. *She* had organised the move from America, *she* had done most of the house-hunting, *she* had taken care of all the details, *she* had arranged Karen's schooling – she had done all the things he ought to have been responsible for.

That damned cat!

What good did it do a man to know he had brains? How could academic knowledge make up for loss of *maleness*? This was what had attracted him to Branksheer in the first place, that drunken old pox-ridden lecher, at home with Ovid or a London whore, a *complete* man.

He decided to write the gift cards. Louise had also left a list of Christmas gifts for Jeremy and Sophia and the three children, Roger, Kevin and Amy. For Roger, he noted again, they'd brought a baseball bat which he'd said was stupid considering the boy would never be able to use it. Louise had said it would be a novelty.

He tried to think of something funny to put on the card

32

but his mind kept going back to days when he was that age and life's great worry was whether you could swing that bat well enough to make the Little League team in Shore Park.

He felt like heaving his typewriter through the window.

As they searched the thick, overgrown hedges for holly with berries, Louise tried to tell Karen something of what it meant to her to be walking once again in an English country lane at Christmas-time.

Karen listened dutifully but she didn't really care.

"Mother, do I have to go to this party?" she asked, when Louise had just finished describing the magic Christmasses of her girlhood.

"Why Karen, you'll love the party. All the boys and girls from round about will be there. It's a chance for you to make some new friends. Don't you want to go?"

"I know I won't like *their* party."

"But whyever not?"

"They only play with each other. They don't like me because I'm American."

"That's nonsense, Karen. It's just that you're new, you've only arrived. They take time to make new friends in the country."

"I wish we were back home. I *hate* Bobby Hedden."

So she still hadn't got over that, Louise thought. They'd enrolled Karen at the Compton Wakley primary school, to which a bus took the local children every morning. Bobby Hedden and two other older children also went in the bus to Compton Wakley, where they got a service bus to the County School. One night Karen had come home crying. It was difficult to get it out of her but eventually she'd said that Bobby Hedden was a bully and tormented the younger children. She said he'd kicked her ankle.

"Why didn't you tell the driver? Mr. Hodgson would stop Bobby if you told him."

"He doesn't care to tell Bobby Hedden *anything*."

This had happened a second time and Louise went to see Mrs. Hedden, thinking this preferable to George's suggestion that he should have it out with Tom Hedden. Bobby's mother was a harassed, tired-eyed woman struggling to make dinner for her large family. The farm seemed to Louise to be in a ruinous state and the small, low-ceilinged kitchen in which

33

the Heddens apparently spent most of their time was a terrible mess, with clothes lying in heaps on every flat surface, hungry cats lurking and darting under the table, several blackened pots pouring out steam from an old-style range.

Louise might have still had the courage to mention Bobby's bullying but while she was thinking of a tactful way to bring the subject up little Janice Hedden had thrown a tantrum.

She'd been sitting at the table, a girl of Karen's age, dirty hair in straggly plaits, jam on her cheeks, snot under her nose, licking her fingers each time she pulled them out of a jar of raspberry jelly.

"Janice, you're makin' a right mess," Mrs. Hedden said occasionally, without taking away the jam jar or wiping the girl's face. Louise had heard that Janice Hedden was, as they said in the village, afflicted, although she didn't know what this meant exactly. Suddenly she threw the jam jar across the table. It rolled over the edge and smashed on the stone floor. Louise had never liked the sound of breaking glass and she had almost cried out.

"Oh Janice!" said Mrs. Hedden, wearily bending down to pick up the pieces and wipe up the jam, at which one of the cats was already licking.

As though she had been struck violently little Janice began to scream. Her face contorted, her eyes closed, she filled the dark kitchen with piercing screams. Louise blinked. The noise seemed to cut right through her head. Mrs. Hedden dropped the glass fragments into a bucket. Only then did she attend to Janice.

"Stop that silly yellin' now," she said. Janice screamed even louder, drawing in great breaths, her little body heaving in a way that made Louise feel like crying. Mrs. Hedden picked her up and carried her through a doorway which Louise presumed led to their bedrooms. Through the small window over the kitchen sink she could see the roof of her blue Zephyr. She felt embarrassed. Mrs. Hedden came back from the other part of the house, Janice's screams still faintly audible.

"Will she be all right? I'm afraid I must have frightened her, I know what they're like at that age with strangers."

"Oh, it wasn't you," said Mrs. Hedden, weary yet patient. "It's one of her fits, that's all."

"What causes them, do you know?"

"The doctors called it somethin', I can't remember the right
34

name of it. She's never been right like. They say she might get over it in time – I don't think they know no better than we do. Tom wanted her put away in a home but they said she ain't bad enough to go in one of they places. Sometimes she's all right. You get used to her."

It was impossible to bring up her complaint about Bobby. Louise left. No reason for her visit was given or asked. The next time the bus came for Karen she had a word with Mr. Hodgson, the driver.

'Them Heddens is all the same," he said, shrugging. "I know what I'd *like* to do to them."

"But you will try to see Bobby doesn't bully the younger ones?" Louise asked. "It's too bad, I can't have my child coming home crying."

"Kids are always fighting or something," said Mr. Hodgson. "I tell 'em but they take no heed."

Still, Louise thought he would probably try to keep an eye on Bobby in future – and there was always the happy thought that Bobby was leaving school at Christmas. She persuaded George that it would be ridiculous for them to stop Karen using the bus because of what was only childish bickering. George had been very bad-tempered.

"If it happens again I'll go to the headmistress," he said. "And if she won't do something I'll drive Karen to school myself. What's wrong with these people, they think children are cattle or something?"

"It's important Karen isn't made to feel different from the others," was Louise's clinching argument. She knew George. Like most Americans, even sophisticated ones, he had a *horror* of that sort of thing.

When she did see a few berries the birds had missed, Louise tried to jolly Karen into some kind of enthusiasm, but neither of them could reach the branch through the tangle of thorns.

"I'm sure you'll soon grow to like it here," she said to Karen as they walked home through the snow. Even as she spoke she noticed the sun had disappeared in a thick, dull sky.

"Mother, who would do that to our cat?" Karen asked.

Louise had hoped this had been forgotten.

"I don't know, darling, we can get another cat. I'll race you to the house."

After lunch, which they ate quietly, each seemingly preoccupied, George said he was going back to his study.

"I thought we'd wrap up the presents," Louise said.

"You and Karen can do that, I really must work," said George, rising from the kitchen table.

"Can't you leave silly old Branksheer for an hour or two – at Christmas?" she replied, irritation in her voice. It was like him, to disappear whenever there was any unpleasantness in the air.

"He isn't silly, honey," said George, with his annoyingly pleasant voice, the one he used when he was at his most sanctimonious. "He's our whole reason for being here."

"He isn't *my* reason. I've got a lot of things to do for Jeremy and Sophia coming. If you don't want to wrap presents why don't you and Karen take a walk up to the Knapmans? I said we'd collect our turkey today."

"I'm behind with my work as it is, Louise, I –"

"Oh God, can't you forget your work for *once*? It's Christmas on Friday, or had you forgotten?"

"Of course I haven't forgotten, honey. I'm going to lose three or four days' working time as it is, I really should get on with –"

"Oh, for heaven's sake! Can't you behave like a normal father and forget that damned book of yours!"

"So that's what you think? Branksheer's some kind of joke? And what d'you mean, behave like a normal father? Don't you think I'm a normal father? I was a normal enough father before we stranded ourselves in this God-forsaken hole!"

The row flared quickly and violently. Each thought there was something irrational about the other.

"I know why you wanted us to come here," George said, his mouth tightened, his anger channelled, as usual, into heavy sarcasm. "You think you're getting old, you're suffering from some delayed adolescent fantasy, aren't you, let's go back to England and re-live the jolly old past. Let's look for romance!"

"What's that bullshit supposed to mean?"

"Karen – you go on out and play or something," said George. They waited till she left, Louise wondering if a good slap on the bottom would shake her daughter out of this unnatural solemnity. What was *wrong* with her?

"Now then, Louise," said George, looking set to play the heavy husband. "I've told you about using that kind of language in front of Karen, I –"

"You've told me! Who do you think you are, you pompous bastard? I'll swear if I bloody well like."

"Not in front of Karen. It doesn't become you, anyway."

"Become me, become me! You sound like Queen Victoria. Hmmph, for a so-called professor you've got a very old-fashioned imagination, haven't you?"

"A so-called professor! That's better than being a so-called poet. I suppose you're just eating your heart out for that fat slob."

"Are you referring to Patrick Ryman? If so, I –"

"Who else would I be referring to? That's why you wanted us to come to this precious little country of yours, isn't it? Romantic fantasy. Did you think he'd come riding up the lane and carry you off? Come to England, I want to show you *my* country! Horseshit! All you wanted was to indulge some sordid little romantic daydream."

"Oh, clever, clever. You found another word for fantasy, You're improving."

"Fantasy suits you."

"Suits *me*? You live in a great non-stop bloody fantasy and you think everybody else is the same. God, you're *sick*."

"Now look here, I didn't start all this, what do –"

"You didn't start it, oh no, you're too damned clever for that. You provoke me into starting it, don't you? Very clever."

"I didn't provoke you! I was perfectly happy, I –"

"Were you hell! You've been brooding all bloody morning. What's eating you now then, your virility problem or whatever the stupid American euphemism is?"

"What do you mean, stupid American? Listen to me, Louise, what's all this really about?"

"It's about you keeping your nose buried in that dreary old book you're supposed to be writing and me having to try and amuse *our* daughter. You're her father, remember? I suppose you think it's beneath your masculine dignity to take an interest in your own child."

"I do take an interest in her."

"Not like a proper father –"

"Not like an English father, you mean? Listen to me, Louise, I –"

"Why do you always tell me to listen to you? I'm not some idiot student on a football scholarship, you know."

"Look, Louise, I'm getting tired of this. Being in England

37

hasn't made you happy, has it? All I get is this anti-American stuff. If you were so keen on England why didn't you marry some faggot Englishman instead of a stupid American?"

"God, if only –"

"If only, if only. I know what's bothering you, Louise. You're worrying about old age creeping up on you *again*. Oh, la-di-da, poor little Louise's all sad and sore, life isn't turning out the great romantic day-dream after all, is it? You poor dear."

"What do you know about romance, you *swot*? You live in your bloody books, that's all you know."

"You knew what I did for a living before you married me. Now you think you'd like a change. Well don't take it out on me, Louise, no woman's going to break my balls –"

"Oh, God, you're so *trite*." She felt the strength for argument draining away. It was all so stupid and futile. "That's a very stupid expression. Why can't Americans stick to castration like everybody else?"

She had hoped she was making a joke. She wasn't. They stared at each other, as though out of breath.

"I didn't realise you'd gone off America so strongly," George said at last. Neither had she.

"Now I know why you didn't ask your mother down here for Christmas," he went on. "You were frightened she'd scare me off this damn country altogether, weren't you?"

She shrugged. For all she despised women who cried unfairly in arguments, she found tears coming to her eyes. She realised she never wanted to go back to America.

"You don't think I'm going to settle down and live here permanently, do you?" He sounded more surprised than angry.

"Do what you bloody like," she said, getting up and walking quickly out of the kitchen. She ran up the stairs and slipped the bolt on the inside of the bathroom door. There she stared in the mirror at a face which rapidly became tear-bloated. She sobbed convulsively for all the things she'd missed.

"Oh Patrick, oh Patrick," she moaned.

When he'd seen Henry Niles safely undressed and put on the bed for the doctor's examination, Pawson told the nurse he'd be in Sister Grady's office.

"Be good now, Henry," he said to Niles, who nodded seriously. Pawson looked at the thin little legs and the pale, bony body and wondered, as he had done many times before, how such a skinny little streak of nothing could have done the terrible things Henry Niles had once done.

He walked through the doors of the clinic where Henry had his weekly kidney injections and crossed the tiled landing to Ward Four.

"Hullo, Kate," he said, leaning his head round the corner of the office door. "Time for tea, is it?"

"You're too early," said the small woman in the blue nursing uniform and starched cap. She didn't look thirty-nine, he thought.

"You know I don't come for the tea, it's you I want to drink in." He entered the office and sat down.

"Is it all right if I rest my aching feet?" he asked, groaning. "Don't think of me as a gentleman caller, I'm more your walking wounded."

"Tuts tuts, you poor old thing," she said, her voice noticeably Irish, a small woman with a clean, clear skin and dark blue eyes. A little beauty! Proud with it, too. But what woman worth chasing ever did give a man an easy time?

"My patient's having his weekly miracle shot," he said. "Looks like a White Christmas, doesn't it? They have White Christmas in Ireland?"

"We don't have time for such nonsense here," she said. "This isn't Two Waters, you know. We've hardly got time to look out of the window."

"Ah begorrah, don't give us all that old blarney. I'm in the nursing business meself, you know. I'm a sister, too. Next year I might be made up to matron. Anyway, you know what they say about nurses, we know what it's all about."

"Ah yes, that's what men with dirty minds say about nurses."

"I suppose so. They've never said it about me."

How did you get round to asking a woman like Kate Grady to go out with you when you were a married man, he wondered for the ten millionth time. She liked him a bit, he knew that, there weren't many people she encouraged to sit in her office.

"And who've you brought today from the snakepit?" she asked.

"Now, now, we don't like that sort of thing. We're very progressive, you know. As it happens there's just the one maladjusted personality today, one of our oldest and best-loved favourites, straight from a successful season at Bedlam, good old Henry Niles. Remember him?"

She made a grimace and seemed to shudder.

"How could I ever forget him? It makes me feel nervous just having a creature like that in the hospital. Shouldn't you be watching him in case he ... I mean, there's a children's ward on the next floor."

"Ah, Henry's past all that," he said, grinning. "His day is over. I don't think he even remembers he's a killer. When we got him he had the mind of an eight-year-old child, you know? I think he's regressed since then. Oh yeah, life would be easy if he was the worst we had to handle."

For all her starchy perkiness and brisk competence he knew she was like everybody else. They pretended to be horrified but they were mad keen to ask questions about what went on in Two Waters.

"But how can they tell when a case isn't dangerous any more?"

"I think they just guess, like the rest of us. You should have a look at him, he's nothing any more. Pathetic. If he wasn't Henry Niles they'd probably be thinking of letting him out. But the public wouldn't stand for it. They've got long memories for that kind of thing. By the way, I've been wanting to ask you this before, how would you like to go out with me some night? We could drive somewhere, a pub, or go to the pictures, whatever you fancy. We could discuss the latest trends in progressive medicine. ..."

His voice lost confidence.

"Oh," she said, looking at the papers she'd been working on. "This is a bit sudden, isn't it?"

"Course it isn't. You know very well it isn't."

"Are you sure you're in a position to take somebody out?"

"Oh, so you've found out then." He smiled without having intended to smile. "You've been checking up on me?"

"Oh no, I just happened to hear somebody say you were married, that's all."

"I see, just casual information. Well, it's true."

"She doesn't understand you, is that it?"

"No, she understands me too bloody well. You won't believe this, but we've lived together in that house for eighteen months and we haven't said a word to each other. Not a word

40

in eighteen months! Notes. We pass notes. I'd often read about things like that, suddenly I realised it's *us*."

"Why don't you leave?"

"It's difficult, isn't it? She won't leave and I've got to stay in the house, there's nothing else at the institution. We're sort of stuck."

"But why do you want to go out with me? I'm no young thing."

"I fancy you, I always have." He put his hand on his nose, as though trying to hide behind it. "I could have left but I'm a coward, I suppose. I want to get a divorce, though. Would you marry me if I got a divorce?" She made a little face, looking down at her papers. He'd made a fool of himself. He felt his face going red. "Didn't you ever think it was funny, me always coming with the Wednesday run, me being a senior nurse? It was to see you, that's why. Anyway, I'm sorry I –"

"Don't be sorry. I'm off tonight as it happens. You could wait for me down the road, at the corner, you know, where the garage is?"

"You mean, you will?"

"For a nurse you took a long time to ask."

For grown-up people they were both ridiculously nervous, he thought.

"It isn't only the inmates who're daft," he said. "I thought you'd probably report me to the Superintendent."

"I've always wanted to go out with a matron," she said.

He wanted to take hold of her hand.

"I'll have to get back to Two Waters and see Henry put away and then get back to the house and change and get the car – I could be back by half-past six. Is that all right?"

"Watch the roads, won't you? I think they said they'll freeze up tonight, even if there isn't any more snow. Maybe we should put it off till another –"

"Not on your – I mean, no, I'll be all right. Half-past six."

When he'd had tea he went back to the clinic ward to see if he could hurry them up. He felt like shouting the good news all over the hospital.

It was half-past two. Through the big ward windows he saw the first flakes of snow.

CHAPTER FOUR

Bill Knapman and Charlie Venner left the Dando Inn around half-past three, the new snow already lying about an inch deep on the step at the back entrance. Bill Knapman took a rag from the floor of the car and wiped the windscreen.

"It'll be worse before it gets better," he said to Charlie. They'd had several whiskies with Harry Ware. Neither of them felt like work. "Better come back with me, have a quick drink. I'll better get down the road with the hay for the sheep before it piles up again."

"I'll bet that gang went back to Tom's place," said Charlie. "Tom'll be dishin' up the scrump."

"Worse'n sheep dip, his stuff. Good for strippin' paintwork I reckon."

On the way up the road from Dando Monachorum they saw the American professor's girl walking by herself. She turned her head away as they came alongside her. She wasn't far from home and Bill Knapman decided not to stop and ask her if she wanted a lift.

"What's wrong wi' her then?" asked Charlie.

"Oh girls that age, no understandin' them," said Bill. "The wife's very nice, y'know."

"Aye, her's English. What's he like, I never spoke to him, some do say he wouldn't give you the time of day."

"Keeps to himself, that's right. Not the kind to push himself in. Could be worse. Remember that bloke who had Trencher's couple of year ago, what was his name, Buckteeth hyphen Scratcherley?"

"Buckley-Hitchings? The R. A. F. bloke?"

"Yeah, funny bugger he were, second day he moved in he was up at us, said he'd heard tell I made cider, could he have some? No holdin' him, was there?"

"He didn't last long. Neither will they lot."

"Maybe not. Though her's very nice."

"Aye, her's English."

Karen Magruder thought she might throw a fit of temper and refuse to go to the Christmas party. She knew Bobby

Hedden and his gang would be there and they wouldn't be nice to her. If it hadn't been for what Daddy had said to her before they left home she would have screamed and screamed and *screamed*.

"You might not find things so nice at first in England," he'd said. "You'll have to make new friends. I'm sorry about that but it's going to be a big thrill for your mother. You've got to help to make it nice for her. England's her home, where she was born. She hasn't been home to see it for years and years. I'm counting on you, Karen."

"But this is our home," she'd said.

"Yes, but your mother's first home was in England. She's looking forward very much to showing you all the places she knows. It'll be a big thrill for her. And for you. You'll promise me, won't you, you'll do everything you can to make her vacation as wonderful as it can be?"

"Oh yes. I wish we could take Sue-Anne with us. She's my *real* friend."

Karen kicked the snow. She decided she'd walk back to the house and look at her calendar. If there was time she'd write another letter to Sue-Anne. The last time she'd looked at her calendar there were only eight months before Daddy said they were going home again.

Poor mother. It couldn't have been very nice for her to grow up in England....

Louise Magruder lay trembling on her bed. The words grew louder and louder in her mind ... *I won't go back ... I won't go back....*

Downstairs she could hear the tapping noise of George's typewriter. What a cold-blooded fish he was. What on earth had ever possessed her to marry the bloody man? Her mother had been right, damn her. Marry your own sort, it's best I always say. That was Mummy! She was sure now she'd only married George to show Mummy she had a mind of her own. Of course! The whole thing had been a silly bit of adolescent rebellion. God, she was tired of him. She thought of Patrick....

When George had come home that afternoon and told her they were going to a party for Ryman the poet she had been so annoyed she could have killed him.

"Oh God no! I thought we were going to have a night on our own. Don't you ever get tired of that same bunch of bores?"

43

She could hear the stridency in her own voice, but there was no stopping herself. She didn't care that George was hurt – he was typically American, anything that upset his *wonderful* home and their *wonderful* relationship came as a deep shock. She often thought that every tiff they had was in some way an insult to the American way of life.

"You'll enjoy it," was all he'd said. So smug! Patronising.

"I will not. Can't we ever have one night away from all this bloody togetherness? What's wrong with you, George, d'you think they'll call you a commie if you avoid them for once?"

"Don't be silly." Jesus, always so damned *patient*. "I promised Hal, this guy Ryman's a bit temperamental by all accounts. Hal's relying on you to give him support, you know, both of you being English?"

"Ryman's *Irish*."

"You know what I mean."

"We all look alike to you, is that it?"

"Come on, honey, it won't be that bad."

"If I go I promise you now I'll get bloody drunk."

"What an adolescent thing to say! Of course you won't get drunk. Leave that to the poets."

They'd been married seven years then and she hadn't been home for over two years and one way or the other she was fed up. That was the summer Karen had had her sulking fits.

The Sapersteins had invited just about everybody to meet Patrick Ryman, obviously because Hal thought there was safety in a large crowd, Ryman having established a reputation which travelled the college circuit in advance. She'd never known the Sapersteins to supply so much booze to so many people and that was saying a lot, for any time you went to their house you could count on Hal pumping it into you as though prohibition was coming back. Even George had been known to get a little high at the Sapersteins.

That night George had been almost drunk. They were, as he kept saying, going through a "difficult phase". In other words he was having one of his periodic attacks of virility trouble. Mid-week sex had gone by the board, now he was even having trouble on Saturday nights. He said this was a normal phase, but as far as she was concerned he was suffering from a very common complaint among men. He was tired of her. But would he admit it! Oh no, that would be something like high treason.

44

At first she'd snorted with disbelief when she saw Patrick Ryman, *the* poet. The bow-tie and the rumpled suit – and the hair! For a moment she felt deeply ashamed to be British in the same room. How could a *man* wear his hair like that, all dank and scurfy? No wonder he kept on scratching his head. Apart from the fact that she couldn't remember a single line he'd written, she had no desire to speak to him, none at all. But inevitably they were introduced. She'd had four drinks.

"Did you hire that suit?" she asked, raising her left eyebrow in what she hoped was arrogant disdain. "Or did Dylan Thomas leave it to you in his will?"

"Oh, you're the English woman," he said, smiling boozily. "The wife said I should give all you academics a bit of a show. Dress dirty, Paddy, she says, it's a sure sign of integrity. At home I wear stiff white collars, y'know. It's difficult to know what you cultural parasites want from a visiting genius like myself."

"You'll do," she said, maintaining her disdain. "You should now vomit on the rug – that'll convince them you're authentic."

"I may do that, darling. After all, the man did say to treat this like my own home. Can I get you a drink? Or can you get me a drink? If I move my feet I may fall over."

"Let me," she said. "I'd like to see you on the floor."

"Hang around, dear."

She fetched him a drink from the trolley. The room was crowded, but most people were content, at this stage, to be briefly introduced to Ryman and then to talk among themselves.

"It's like winning the bloody pools," he said, taking a disrespectfully large gulp of Hal Saperstein's Glen Grant.

"What is?" she asked, still antagonistic.

"Coming over here on one of these culture jaunts. One minute there I was at home, a bum with four kids and twenty barmaids to support – the next you're supposed to be Clark Gable. D'you know something, Mrs. – what was it again – Macwhat? Is that supposed to be Scottish? Anyway, whatever your name is, I'll tell you my mother used to tell me to put on clean underwear when I went out of the house, if yese git run down, Pathrick me bhoy yese'll want clean underwear in the infirmary or yese'll make me ashamet o'ye. Jesus Christ our Lord and Saviour, if they saw my underpants they'd deport me. D'yese fancy a look at them yourself like?"

45

"No thank you."

"You show good taste."

After a few more drinks she found herself laughing *with'* him, in spite of herself. Everything he said seemed like a deliberate attempt to make her think he was a human disgrace.

"You've never read any of my stuff? Och, I shouldn't bother between you and me and the gatepost, they're hardly worth the effort, most of the good lines are pinched anyway. Jesus Christ Saviour of Little Children, are all these mighty men gathered here in my name? They must have empty fucking lives."

He went on and on, talking to her as though she was a fellow waster from a Paddington pub. The party became loud and noisy. People stood in the hall and in other rooms. There was coming and going from upstairs. George was nowhere to be seen. People came up to Patrick and said stupid things. She tried not to laugh when he insulted them with carefully polite replies.

"Am I familiar with Graves? Oh sure, most of my best friends are in them right now. Did you ever hear of the paper in Ireland that was reporting this funeral and they said Councillor O'Toole slipped and fell in on top of the coffin and the incident cast a gloom over the subsequent proceedings? You didn't? It's a well-known story. Very evocative, nay redolent."

People smiled energetically and obviously didn't understand him. She felt that they were fellow-conspirators. She later couldn't even remember why it was they decided to go upstairs, but she remembered standing inside a dark room with her back against the wall and Patrick trying to talk her on to the bed. All they did was kiss – it must have been a farcical sight, for she was six inches taller than he was. She remembered him going on and on about how you could get quickie divorces in Mexico City and how he was small and ugly and women didn't like him and his wife hated him because he'd got her pregnant in the first place and he wouldn't drink so much only he was the loneliest man in the world and she was the first truly beautiful woman who'd understood him.

She didn't remember going home with George. In the morning she had a terrible headache. The phone went about ten. Patrick wanted her to come over to his hotel. It was a fantastic effort, in her condition. She'd told herself she was only going to let him know he wasn't as pathetic as he made himself out to be.

Of course she'd known why she was going, feverish with the hangover, so depressed the house seemed like a soundproof cell.

"So there you are, all my sexual tricks from A to B," he said when they finally stopped making love. "I hope you notice I had a shower in your honour? I knew you'd be used to hygienic men. I'd have cut my toe-nails but I've only got the one razor-blade and I need to shave for my audiences. Is it true what they say about these Yanks?"

"What's that?"

"Here, watch it, you shouldn't speak with your mouth full, don't you know any manners at all? You're depraved! No, here, this girl I know, she's telling me these American fellas do it like buck rabbits, up and on and quick batter and off again. Is that right?"

"You could say that."

"For God's sake, woman! Are you hungry or something? Jesus Christ Our Blessed Lord they're funny people over here. Are you still going to Mexico with me?"

"Oh, you remembered?"

"Of course I remembered. I wasn't drunk last night, you know. Sure, your honour, if you thought I was drunk last night you shoulda seen me on Saturday night. No, I'm serious, let's piss off out of this and fly to Mexico. I saw it in a film, quickie divorces. The wife doesn't even have to know."

"You couldn't afford me."

"I never said I could. Could you afford me, that's more like it."

As the drink wore off it began to appear that he was serious, at least by his standards. Her natural impulse was to make jokes about it but there was no knowing with a funny man like him. He seemed so unbalanced.

"I think I might kill myself if it gets any worse," he said at one stage. "I'm a burden to the human race."

"We'd leave five children in broken homes," she said, trying to bring him to reason, if only for the sake of the lunch at which he was to meet so many allegedly important people.

"Och, to hell with the children, I don't like mine all that much if the truth be known. Think of that last moment before you die, you've done all the decent things all your life, you're lying there kicking the bucket – do you think it would matter then?"

47

But she had left the hotel and if George hadn't found one of Patrick's letters she would have made herself forget the whole thing. Not that it was a love letter, more a series of childish jokes. George, however, had taken it badly. What he resented was the fact she could have a secret correspondence with another man. It spoiled his beautiful dream of togetherness. He took it for granted that she hadn't even thought of going to bed with Patrick! That was even more annoying than if he'd gone berserk with jealousy. She told herself that only a very imaginative and intelligent woman could have seen beneath the seedy buffoonery Patrick showed to the world.

And that, she told herself as she lay staring at the ceiling, the unread book lying on her breast, was my big moment. Illicit romance, the only one of my whole life. I should have run away to Mexico with him. It wouldn't have lasted – but I'd have done something wild and selfish – just for me.

Was it too late? Soon even fat little lonely drunks might not want me....

I guess I was in the wrong, George Magruder said to himself, sitting at his desk in the study. Was that 'guess' in the English or American sense? He didn't *think* he was in the wrong. Life would be a whole lot simpler if a man could still put a pernickety wife over his knee and give her backside a roasting. But he wasn't that kind of man, even if Louise had been that kind of woman.

Like many academics he was conscious of, but unable to do anything about, an imbalance between the impressive depth and range of knowledge he had in his special field and the rest of his mental activities. His own secret – and somewhat childish – theory was that there are only so many brain cells and a man who filled an inordinate number of these cells with one subject has less room – literally – for anything else. It was hardly to be expected that one human brain could hold a vast store of information on English literature and then have equal capacity for other commitments of the same intensity.

Einstein, it was said, could not tie his own shoelaces. Nabokov ran about in fields with a butterfly net. A famous critic and lay theologian had a passion for playing croquet in the nude. In his own case, old films took the place of butterflies or seashells. A non-hobby he called it, requiring no more involvement than a good memory and a willingness to sit till after midnight in front of the television.

He could spot famous stars in early bit parts, he could put names to the faces of *second-rate* bit players. Did anybody else in the world have such knowledge of Hollywood's immortal trivia? Stars interested him less than the anonymous faces who had down the years peopled the mechanical dreams from the fantasy production belt. He saw them as prototype personalities of the twentieth century. . . . Elisha Cook (the twisted face of the third gangster, the little man who always cracked under pressure), Robin Raymond, Gloria Dickson, Adele Jergens, Charles Smith, Luis Van Rooten, Percy Helton, Russell Simpson (who stepped out of his grade to play the father in *The Grapes of Wrath*), Don Beddoe, Raymond Walburn, Paul Harvey, John Litel, Tom Kennedy (monopolist of Irish New York cop parts).

If old films were his non-hobby, Westerns were his specialisation. He remembered the plots of innumerable sage-bush sagas starring Roy Rogers (with Dale Evans). He was a connoisseur of second-grade cowboy stars, Rod Cameron, John Payne, Randolph Scott.

There was nothing surprising about all this, he often said – defensively, for there was something embarrassing about comprehensive knowledge of a subject which few other people are aware of.

"Great minds *like* simple things," Louise would say reassuringly, in those days when she was still interested in reassuring him.

"There's a peculiar and unexplored potency to mass subculture," was another of his rationalisations. Yet . . . was John Wayne swapping punches with other giants any more ludicrous a fantasy than Branksheer's bawdy England? Given the choice, wouldn't any man prefer to know he could defend his land and log cabin against Shawnee war parties – instead of being stuck at a desk?

It was not an idea he could ever reveal to the people he worked with. It couldn't stand up to severe analysis, but it was real. It had started as a joke and then grafted itself on to his consciousness; the frontier was no more and a man had to settle for the second-best. Like being a professor.

He couldn't work. He went upstairs. Louise was reading on the bed.

"I want to say I'm sorry," he said.

"What for?" Her voice was huffy, a little girl's voice.

"I'm *sorry*! I lost my temper unnecessarily."

"Did you?"

"Come on, Louise, I've come up to apologise."

"All right, so you've apologised."

"Well?"

"Well what?"

"Don't you want to say anything?"

"No."

"Look, I notice it's always me who makes it up first. Aren't you ever in the wrong, just a little bit in the wrong?"

"Probably."

"Well then –"

"Oh shut up and leave me alone."

"*Please*, Louise, let's not be stupid, huh?"

He sat on the bed and took hold of her right hand, making her drop the book on the bedcover. She stared at him defiantly, as though he was threatening to strike her.

"Don't look at me like that. I'm not going to hit you, silly."

He smiled, as he thought, apologetically. Louise thought it was a coy little smirk.

"That's what's wrong with you."

"What is?"

"You haven't got the guts to hit me. Go on, try it, you'll feel better. I deserve it. Go on."

"Come on, honey, let's not –"

"Don't honey me, you all-forgiving bastard. What do you think being married is, the stupid PTA? God, you make me sick, look at you, all nicey-nicey smiles, you big sook. What's going on in that great All-American head of yours? Eh? Be honest – for once."

"There's no need to –"

"Yes there is. I'm sick of it, the whole thing. What's wrong with you? One minute you're whining and moaning you wish you were a big man – like Hemingway, ha ha, Hemingway's just your type, little Georgie wants to be a grown-up man with a hairy chest! But little Georgie hasn't got the guts to hit his own bitch of a wife."

"All right, I'll smack your teeth on the floor if it makes you any happier."

"Don't smirk at me! You can't get round me that way. My

mother was right, damn her, we should never have got married. I'm no good to you."

"Oh shut up. It's time you were getting Karen ready for the party. You'll get over this, it's only a mood. It's affecting both of us living here. This isn't our house, we hardly own a single thing in it. Maybe we made a mistake coming –"

"No, the mistake was a lot earlier."

"Oh Louise, don't say things like that. You'll only regret them afterwards. I'll go and find Karen."

As usual she felt cheated and enraged. The saintly bastard.

When she and Karen drove away from the house she did not wave or smile to George, who stood on the little path at the front door, watching the car tyres send up little spumes of soft snow. Even after the car had gone out of sight up the lane he still stood there, snowflakes settling on his chest and shoulders. . . .

Frank Pawson told the ambulance-driver he was in a hurry to get back to Two Waters.

"We'll make it by four, easy," said the driver. "I'm in a hurry myself, the road might get blocked up if it starts snowing again."

In the back Henry Niles looked tired.

"You'd better lie down on the bench, Henry my old son," said Pawson. "Have a kip, you'll be home soon. I know, I'll strap you down, you won't get bounced about so much."

"That's a good idea," said Henry Niles, as though he was a small boy being introduced to a new game. As Frank Pawson fastened the buckle he felt like apologising to the poor little bastard. It wasn't fair, was it, the way things turned out for different people? Here he was fair laughing, things couldn't be better, and here was poor old Henry, a lunatic. Never had a chance, poor bastard. Still, Henry was lucky in one way – there was a time when they might have hung him, lunatic or not.

"All right then, Henry? Have a bit of a snooze." He might have been tucking in a baby. He sat back on the other bench and thought about Kate Grady. It had turned out better than he'd hoped. She fancied him, they were at the right age, she was a grown woman and she knew what she was going into, nurses made great wives, life couldn't have turned out better. Christ, wouldn't *her* face be a caution when he told her? He

51

thought of all the brilliantly vicious things he would say, just as he was leaving, pay her back for all her evil. He felt the ambulance moving fast. Put your foot down, matey, don't waste a second. . . .

The ambulance was doing about forty when it came to the left-hand bend at the top of the twisting slope down to Fairwater Ford. It was then the snowflakes began to fly on to the windscreen, hundreds of fast-moving limpets seizing a foothold. Like many professionals, the driver didn't immediately switch on his windscreen-wipers.

When he saw the snow would stick, he flicked the switch. His vision was obscured.

The glass cleared. He was about ten yards past the point where he would normally have slowed down and applied slight brake pressure to go into the bend. He braked.

The ambulance went into a skid. There was no room for him to drive into the skid. Instead of taking the corner to the left, the ambulance slid, side on, at the low bank on the right hand side.

It hit the bank, which was only eighteen inches high. The impact on the offside wheels sent the vehicle toppling, roof first, over the bank. It turned over once – twice – three times – on the steep slope. Then it came to a standstill, resting on its side, half-way down the incline.

It took Henry Niles some moments to understand that he was hanging off the bench with a leather belt round his chest. Pawson lay beneath him, not moving. Henry Niles was confused. The strap made it difficult to breathe.

"Mr. Pawson? It's hurting me."

Pawson lay still. Henry began to whimper. His fingers could make no impression on the metal buckle. He struggled, his legs hanging over Pawson's head. Then he slipped through the belt and fell on top of Pawson. He started to cry. Mister Pawson didn't move. Henry shouted. Nobody came. Sometimes they came when he shouted, sometimes they didn't. The ambulance doors were open, one flap resting on snow. He clambered out, his whimpering stopping when he found his feet in snow.

He remembered it, white and cold and wet. Men had chased him over a big space, he didn't know why they chased him, he'd run and run and run until he'd fallen in it, they were shouting so loudly his ears had almost burst. Then he remembered why they were chasing him. He *did* remember, some-

52

times, but most of the time he was able not to think about it. He knew that men didn't like him.

Many psychiatrists and psychologists and doctors had tried to penetrate the mind of Henry Niles, the mental defective who had murdered three children before, at the age of twenty-five, he'd been put away for the rest of his life in Two Waters. These men had come to an almost unanimous conclusion – that Henry had a mental age of eight. None of them could explain why other humans with the same mental age – children of eight years old, for instance – did not have Henry's deadly compulsion to rape and strangle little girls. Occasionally they detected signs of a more mature intelligence in Henry, but it was impossible to draw him out. With adults he behaved like a frightened child, with children he was a giant ogre. As long as grown-up people were present he tended to cower in corners, like a savagely beaten puppy. But when he was alone in a world of children, he grew up.

He stood alone beside the upturned ambulance. It was nine years since he had been on his own in the fresh air. Back up the slope he saw the other man, the driver, lying in the snow. Sniffing heavily, he started up the slope. Behind him was the great moor, dark now as the snow fell in earnest. He slipped several times as he scrambled up to the driver. He looked down on a face half-pushed into snow. Blood trickled from the ear and moved in a throbbing stream down the man's cheek.

"Gentle Jesus meek and mild," Henry moaned. He began to clamber desperately to the top of the slope. He shouldn't have seen that blood. They would blame him for that. There was blood that other time. It wasn't his fault. He would have to run away before the men came, shouting.

He had walked about half a mile in the snow, down the road to the Fairwater Ford and over the little footbridge beside the ford and half-way up the hill on the other side, before a car pulled up beside them.

"Want a lift then?" said one of three young farm workers in the car. "It's a funny ol' day for walkin'. We can take you's far's Compton Wakley, that suit you?"

"It wasn't my fault," said Henry.

One of the men laughed. Henry looked at him through the open window.

"We ain't blamin' you for walkin'," said the first man. "Got

53

caught, did you? Don't do to risk it on the moor. Changes fast like."

The car made good time to Compton Wakely. The men talked among themselves. Henry was happy. *They* didn't think it was his fault. They were nice men.

At Compton Wakley he stood by the side of the road until the car drove off. Then he began walking down a road marked by a signpost: FOURWAYS CROSS. He had gone only a few hundred yards when another car stopped and a farmer offered him a lift as far as Compton Fitzpaine. He got into the car.

"You'll be goin' to the dance at Dando then?" said the farmer. "You must be dancin' mad to try and walk it on a night like this."

"It wasn't my fault," said Henry.

The farmer snorted.

"It'll be your own fault if you don't get back this night," he said. "I reckons us'll be the last car along this road the way it's comin' down."

"I don't want to go back," said Henry Niles.

"Just as well then," said the farmer. Dances, he thought, always attracted them.

CHAPTER FIVE

George Magruder wandered about the silent house, unable to concentrate on his work, irritated at what he saw now was his own stupidity. In the kitchen he switched on the transistor radio which Louise used when she was cooking. It was some disc-jockey programme, a slimily ingratiating English voice smeared by what the idiot fondly imagined was an American accent. It made him even more irritated. How often in arguments back home had he used the B.B.C. as an example of public-interest broadcasting? Now it sounded like a third-rate copy of the worst kind of American huckstering.

He heard the disc-jockey say news time was approaching. He walked through to the dining-room and then into the sitting-room. What he missed was people. This was life in a vacuum. The sooner he could wrap up Branksheer the sooner they would leave this place.

Behind, in the empty kitchen, the news-reader gave details of a new wage freeze. Then . . .

"Henry Robert Niles is missing from an ambulance which crashed while taking him to Two Waters. Niles, who was found guilty but insane at two separate murder trials ten years ago – one after he'd escaped and murdered a third child – was being taken from Trebovir County Hospital. At a public inquiry into his escape it was stated that he had a mental age of eight and would never be allowed to leave a maximum security institution. Police say snow and bad visibility on Tornmoor are hampering their search. Niles is wearing a white shirt, brown jacket and grey trousers. Two other men are reported to be critically injured after the crash. . . ."

In the sitting-room George Magruder punched his right fist into the palm of his left hand. He decided he would walk down to the school. It was ridiculous to stay cooped up here, like some neurotic in the early stages of paranoia. Maybe in a crowd Louise would be more reasonable.

He put on the old rubber boots in the kitchen. The news reader said heavy snow would continue through the night in the west. He switched off the radio. Nothing like the jolly old British to tell you the obvious. It was snowing heavily outside. They probably made up their weather forecasts by looking out of the window.

He took his nylon jacket from a hook, zipped up the front and pulled the parka-hood over his head, tying the strings under his chin.

"Here we go, one man against the primeval elements," he said, out loud, as he slammed the door. "A hundred miles to Nome and the wolves are howling for food. On – into the raging blizzard."

By the time he reached the end of the lane, his head bent to protect his face against the driving snow, he was engaged in a fantasy which was a combination of Chaplin's *Gold Rush* and a James Stewart film, the name of which, for the moment, escaped him. . . .

The children's party was so happy Louise felt like crying. The Rev. and Mrs Hood had met everybody at the door, shaking hands and giving out sweets.

"And this is Karen, that's your name, isn't it?" said the curate, bending slightly, his hands on his knees, smiling into Karen's face. "Merry Christmas, Karen, I'm sure you'll have a lovely time with all these lovely boys and girls."

"Say Merry Christmas to Mr and Mrs Hood, Karen." Louise smiled at the curate and his wife. "This is the first time Karen's been to a Christmas party in England."

"You must tell us about Christmas in America, Karen," said Mrs Hood. Mr Hood patted her head. Karen ducked away. "Don't be shy now, we're all friends here."

Louise saw Mrs Jean Knapman and two other women standing at the head of the long trestle table on which the children's cakes and oranges were already laid, a Christmas cracker by each plate.

Jean Knapman introduced Louise to Mrs Venner and Mrs Hedden.

"We've already met," Louise said to Bobby Hedden's mother. Mrs Hedden smiled briefly. Louise was very glad of Jean Knapman's friendliness, for she had been a little nervous about the party. She had the feeling they were not particularly popular in the village.

Small boys were already racing up and down the centre of the hall. At first the girls tended to stay by their mothers, but soon little groups began to form.

"You sit beside Karen, Lucy," Jean Knapman said to her daughter when the Rev. Hood announced that it was time to take places for tea. Louise watched Karen walking shyly to the table. There was something almost sad about little girls of that age, something solemn and proud. Or was she just feeling sad herself?

"Come on, Janice," said Mrs Hedden. "You like cake, don't you?"

"Isn't it a shame?" said Louise as they watched Mrs Hedden lead Janice to the table. "Isn't there any chance she'll ever be any better?"

"The doctors don't seem to think so," said Jean Knapman. "The Heddens wanted her put in one of they homes but there wasn't no room, not when she was just a baby. Now, well, it would be terrible, wouldn't it, to take her away from what she knows?"

Louise felt a strong upsurge of pity for the little girl with the blank face. Why should an innocent child have its life taken away before it had started? She wanted to cry at the stupidity of it all.

After tea, eaten in a rising crescendo of noise from the two lines of children, the mothers cleared the trestle tables of dirty paper cups and plates and crumbs. Children stampeded up and down the small hall. Louise was glad to see that Lucy Knapman and Karen seemed to have made friends. They sat together when forms were pushed in front of the small stage, where the Rev. Hood made a small speech about the meaning of Christmas and then introduced Mr Hankinson, the conjurer.

Little girls sat with wide eyes and open mouths, little boys ooohed, older boys muttered and giggled and jostled each other, their heads down in subversive conspiracy. Mr Hankinson tore newspapers and magically made them whole again. He told weak jokes as he lifted his left trouser leg to show a red sock and his right trouser leg to show a black sock. He dropped his trouser legs and when he lifted them again the socks had changed over. Louise tried to think how he had done it. Was it one of those small boys who'd strangled their cat? She frowned. All day she'd been trying to forget the cat. Somebody must have come up their lane at night. It was the sort of thing small boys did. What small boys were out after dark on a night of heavy snow? Maybe the cat had wandered – chased hens. That could be it, it had been caught by someone and that was their way of telling strangers not to let their cats run wild. It was too preposterous, nobody would be so warped.

A trick with a glass of water under a Chinese box did not turn out so well. As Mr Hankinson lifted the box with a sweeping gesture – presumably to reveal the glass of water mysteriously emptied – he knocked it on to the floor. The children roared with laughter as he blushed and bent down to pick up the fragments. Louise winced. It was one of those stupid, irrational childhood things, she knew that, but she just could not stand the sound of glass breaking. Once she'd been to a cowboy picture with George and they'd been shooting at empty bottles on a fence and she'd almost been sick.

After the conjurer the mothers went among the children with Christmas crackers left unpulled by the younger children. Jean Knapman gave one to her Lucy and one to Karen.

"Why don't you let little Janice pull your cracker, Karen?" said Louise. Karen made a face. "Go on, she wants some fun, too, you know."

Karen and Lucy went over to where Mrs Hedden sat with

her arm round Janice's shoulders. When Mrs Hedden saw what the two girls wanted to do, she was almost pathetic in her blushing gratitude.

The three women talked together for a few moments, until they heard Janice screaming. They turned to see what had happened. Janice had one end of a cracker and was trying to hold it against her chest, yelling when Lucy and Karen tried to take hold of the other end.

"She doesn't understand," Mrs Hedden apologised. They went over to the little girls. They told Karen and Lucy to pull one cracker to show Janice what she was meant to do. Janice refused to give up her cracker. Louise sensed that the other women in the hall were looking unsympathetically. They probably didn't like the idea of Janice being there at all. She felt the need to make some gesture. She sat down beside Janice and put her arm round her shoulders.

"It's all right, darling," she said, "we're not going to take it away from you."

Janice stopped screaming, but she held on to the cracker.

"Santa Claus will be here in a moment," said Jean Knapman to the girls. They'd seen the Rev. Hood leave to change into the Santa suit. "I wonder what'll he have for you from the tree."

Children were already crowding round the tree in the corner near the door.

"Why don't you and Lucy take Janice to see Santa Claus, Karen?" said Louise. "Take care of her, won't you?"

"I should go with her," said Mrs. Hedden, doubtfully.

"They'll be all right," said Jean Knapman. "Lucy is very responsible for her age."

Louise was on the point of saying that Karen was just as responsible as Lucy, but she stopped herself.

They watched the three little girls walk to the edge of the crowd, trying to find a gap in the semi-circle of excited children.

"Time for a cup of tea!" said Jean Knapman. She introduced Louise to some of the other mothers who stood at the opposite end of the hall from the Christmas tree, enjoying a brief respite. For the first time Louise felt there was a chance of becoming part of the life of Dando Monachorum. She but wished there was some way George could be introduced in the same way. Maybe she could ask Jean Knapman if her husband wouldn't take George down to the Inn some night. It was *very* important – to be introduced by someone the villagers accepted as one of their own.

The scream rang out above the hubbub. The mothers turned, cups held between saucers and mouths. There was another scream. Then they saw the door open and slam shut. Santa Claus had just stepped among the crowd of children, like a man wading through a field of corn. He stopped, his hooded head turned to the door. Some of the mothers sensed trouble. It took them some moments to push through the press of clamouring children. Neither Lucy nor Karen were to be seen.

'Where's my Janice?" Mrs Hedden asked the children. They didn't seem to hear her in the excitement of Santa's arrival. Louise shoved children aside to reach the door. The small porch was cold – and empty.

She opened the outside door, a blast of wind smacking her face, snow whirling into the little vestibule. Jean Knapman and Mrs Hedden came behind her.

They went out into the miniature storm of snowflakes that danced under the light above the porch door.

"Karen! Karen!"

Louise ran across the playground, the soles of her boots slipping on hard-trodden snow. The three mothers stood in the road, shouting the names of their daughters. Then Karen and Lucy appeared, two small shapes out of the driving snow.

"Oh, Mummy, Janice ran out and we couldn't see where she went," said Lucy.

"She was frightened when Santa came in," said Karen. "We couldn't stop her."

The three mothers ran a few yards either way up the road but it was dark and as soon as they were out of range of the school lights, the darkness was solid, a cold wall of downpouring snow. Jean Knapman ran back to her car for the torch in the dashboard compartment. Mrs Hedden stood in the middle of the road, shouting "Janice! Janice!" Jean Knapman ran to the nearest cottage.

Karen Magruder burst into tears.

The first police car which attempted the road from Compton Wakley to Fourway Cross struggled for a mile down the narrow lane before it ran into a wheel-high drift and came to a halt. The two constables got out of the white Mini and decided there was no hope of pushing on. The wind plastered their uniforms white as they bent their backs and strained to shove the Mini backwards out of the drift. They radioed that they were turning back.

At Compton Wakley Police Station it was decided that it didn't matter. Henry Niles was in bad health and even a strong man would have had great difficulty in getting off the Moor in that kind of weather. They decided to put car patrols on the main roads on both sides of the Moor so that he couldn't cross over and lose himself in the rabbit warren of narrow lanes and small villages of Dando. Other police cars drove up and down the road across the Moor until fast-falling snow made this impossible.

"You'd have to feel sorry for the poor bugger," said a police sergeant staring at snowflakes eddying thickly in the beam of the headlights. "He'll freeze to death."

"Won't be much of a loss," said the constable. "Lunatics like that shouldn't be in a position to get out."

"You'd hang him, would you?"

"Maybe not hang him. An injection. He's a liability – to himself much as anything."

"The Two Waters folk say he's not dangerous any more. Bad health."

"Can't be bad enough for my taste. You ever see the photographs of the kids he done in? Gave me nightmares for months, they did."

"Aye, I know. But he's no better than a kid himself. He isn't responsible."

"That'd be a lot of comfort to they kids. And their mothers."

In the morning, it was decided, policemen and soldiers could make a sweeping search of the part of the Moor where the ambulance had crashed.

"I don't suppose we'll find the body till the snow melts," said an inspector. "They say you die peaceful enough when it's this cold. Just go to sleep in the snow."

It seemed an ideal solution. . . .

When George Magruder walked towards the door of the school two men stopped him.

"It's that American from Trencher's," said one.

60

"What's going on?" asked George. "Why are you looking at me like that?"

"You better get your wife and kid home quick's you can," said the other. "Niles the maniac's escaped from Two Waters."

"He could help look for Janice Hedden," said the first man.

"What's going on?" George demanded. "I want to see my wife."

"Little Janice Hedden's disappeared," said the other man. George didn't understand. He pushed past them into the porch. Opening the inner door he was confronted by groups of white, strained faces.

"What's going on?" he asked Louise. She told him about Janice Hedden.

"Mr Hood's gone to phone round the nearest farms," she said. "We need search parties but the mothers won't leave their children."

"I'll drive you back to the house," he said. "The road may be blocked if we wait much longer. I'll come back and help them once I've got you and Karen safe home. Come on."

"I should stay and help. Mrs Hedden's in a terrible state. They're fetching the doctor."

"There's plenty of people to help her. Just get Karen and let's go. Some maniac has escaped from Two Waters."

He was speaking loudly and she felt conspicuous.

"Everybody else is waiting," she said, quietly, pulling him close by clutching the elbow of his jacket. "They'll think it funny us going off."

"Don't argue. It'll look funnier if I go off on my own. Do you want to walk two miles in this damn snow?"

Trying to avoid the faces of the other women, she told Jean Knapman that they were going home and that George would be coming back to join the search parties. Jean Knapman said it was the best thing they could do, but Louise felt ashamed. They were the only people leaving the hall. Karen sat between them in the car. The clicking of the windscreen wipers formed an insistent rhythm which seemed to grow louder and louder as their mutual silence lengthened. At last Louise could no longer keep her temper bottled up.

"I don't appreciate you being bossy in public," she said.

"Bossy? With some sex-maniac on the loose and the road closing up? Use your commonsense, Louise, you –"

"Don't talk to me about commonsense, you bastard!"

"Louise! Not in front of Karen!"

"Yes, in front of Karen, it's time she knew, there's no use letting her grow up in a bloody dream-world. You had to come and spoil everything, didn't you, just as –"

"Louise, for the last time, will you –"

The snow was a steeply-angled cascade of white feathers. Out of it, into the beam of the headlights, came the figure of a man.

Instinctively Louise grabbed Karen with both arms.

"George!"

She felt a bump. George shouted something she didn't catch. He stopped the car.

"We hit him, we hit him, I couldn't stop at that distance, I couldn't –"

"For God's sake! Get out and see what's happened!"

She and Karen watched through the windscreen as George walked round to the front of the car, his shoulders hunched against wind and snow. He bent down out of sight. Then he stood up and shouted. Louise opened her door, immediately shivering with a cold whip of wind on her legs. George came round towards her.

"Back up," he called. "He's underneath. Back up about a yard."

She pulled Karen across her lap and got behind the wheel. The thought of getting the wrong gear made her feel even more hysterical. The car seemed to jump backwards. George waved. George bent down and they saw him come up with the dark shape in his arms. Staggering slightly he came round to the rear door. Louise leaned back to open it from the inside. George struggled to lift the man on to the back seat. Louise twisted round, trying to see his face.

"Is he –"

"We'd better get him to the house, I don't think I hit him too hard."

"Who is he?"

"I don't know. Let's go, huh?"

Once or twice the car looked as though it might stick in snow but by reversing and starting forward again Louise forced it through the drifts.

"His eyes are open," George said from the back seat. "I'll carry him inside, you get the car into the garage. Karen, you stay in the car till your mother parks it."

As he carried the man – who was almost worryingly light – up the path, George tried to remember what he knew about First Aid, but the only lesson he could remember from the Boy Scouts was not to move an injured person. The man was so light he was able to hold him up with one arm while he felt for the keys. Then he picked him up and carried him in both arms into the sitting-room, where he laid him on the couch.

Louise came in.

"I couldn't get the garage doors open, there's so much snow lying," she said.

"It doesn't matter, we won't be going anywhere in the car. Look, his eyes are open but he doesn't seem to be looking at anything."

"Is he breathing?"

"Yeah. I don't think I hit him too hard, not hard enough to knock him out."

"How could you tell?"

"I just *know*, that's all. We'd better get those clothes off him, he's *wet*. What the hell was he doing out in the snow without a coat? Louise, get some blankets, will you?"

"Shouldn't we give him brandy – or something?"

"In a minute. Karen, see to the fire, will you? Turn it all the way up."

Karen seemed ready to burst into tears. Since coming into the sitting-room she'd stood on one spot in the middle of the floor.

"The fire, Karen!"

She turned the air gauge up to eight, its limit, and worked the lever which shook dead ash into a tray. Louise ran upstairs and pulled blankets off one of the spare beds. Her hands trembled.

When she went downstairs George had pulled off the man's shoes and socks and trousers and was unfastening the buttons of his shirt. When he was down to his vest and pants – which to Louise's relief seemed quite clean – he rubbed the man's thin legs and small, white feet with a bathroom towel. Louise kept thinking she'd have to wash the towel and the blankets. She could hear her mother – library books and coins and strange men, they were dirty, they carried germs and disease. The little man's mouth opened and closed several times, but his eyes showed no life. George tucked the blankets round his body and under his feet.

63

"I'll phone the doctor," he said. "I don't know what we should give him to drink. There isn't any brandy anyway."

"There's whisky and gin – and some sherry."

George grinned.

"He might like ice with it. You'd better hang up his clothes in the drying cupboard."

"I'm not touching *his* clothes."

"All right, I'll do it."

The drying cupboard was upstairs in the bathroom. As he shook out the man's clothing, George tried to give Louise the benefit of the doubt. He was sure she hadn't always been like this, yet when he tried to think of what she *was* like before he couldn't remember the actuality. The man's jacket was a wet, cold lump. He opened it out and shoved his hand down the sleeve, to turn it inside out. Maybe some farm-worker dressed up in his best. Clean enough. His eye was caught by a white patch on the inside of the collar. He pulled the sleeve out and held up the jacket to look at the patch. The white material was soggy and wet and for a moment he couldn't make out what letters were formed by the red cotton stitches.

He moved over to the light.

He saw then. The stitching made five, run-on letters.

NILES.

Niles?

Niles the –?

He heard footsteps on the stairs. Where was Karen?

"Louise!" he shouted, running to the bathroom door.

CHAPTER SIX

He pushed past Louise on the stairs, ducking his head as he came down through the sitting-room doorway.

Louise was behind him.

"George! Have you gone mad?"

Karen was at the window, her head bent so that her face was hidden. The man lay still, as before, on the sofa.

"Karen?" He walked across. She wouldn't look up. He took her head in both hands and lifted her face up. She was crying.

"What's wrong, honey?"

64

Karen shook her head.

"Don't cry, Karen! Daddy's here. He won't hurt you."

"What do you mean? What's up with you, George?'

He turned on Louise.

"Can't you stop being hysterical for a moment?"

"I'm not hysterical! Why did you run down the stairs? Who's going to hurt Karen?"

Their little girl began to cry out loud. If ever he had fought any impulse in his life it was nothing compared to the effort of not smacking Louise across the face.

"I want you to phone the doctor," he said, his hand on Karen's shoulder, his face grimly composed, as though he was trying to will Louise to calm down.

"Why are you crying, Karen?" Louise asked.

"She doesn't like all this bickering," he said. "Louise, I want you to phone the doctor – now. Tell him we ran this guy down in the road, he may be injured internally. I'll take Karen upstairs."

He could not be sure that Karen wouldn't have heard Niles' name at the school. It was important she shouldn't know who he was. He put his hand on Louise's upper arm, pressing tight, speaking deliberately, hoping the seriousness would communicate itself.

"It's urgent, Louise. That man may be bleeding to death inside. I don't want any arguments. Come on, Karen."

He took his daughter's hand as they climbed the stairs.

"Now then, honey, you wash your face and brush your teeth, you'll need plenty of sleep, we'll be up late all through Christmas. I'll go and plug in your electric blanket."

When she turned on the water, too occupied with her unhappiness to argue with him, he slipped the big key out of the lock on the bathroom door. He closed the door and turned the key. Maybe she wouldn't hear. If she did he could say he'd been playing a game. He went quickly and quietly down the stairs, avoiding the third step from the top, the one that cracked loudly when stepped on.

Niles was still. He went into the little hall, where the telephone stood on the window ledge. Louise was looking in the telephone directory for the Allsopps' number.

"I've got to tell you something, Louise," he began. Her face was hostile. "Please try to think of Karen before you indulge in any hysterics. It doesn't matter what's eating us, think of her."

"What is it?"

"For God's sake keep a grip on yourself. You know who that man is? I'm going to tell you, Louise. And if you even start to make a noise I'm going to slap you hard. Do you understand?"

She stared, a mixture of resentment and disbelief.

"That man is Henry Niles, the maniac. His name's written inside his coat."

"Niles? I don't believe –"

"I meant it, I'll give you such a smack, Louise! It's Niles, all right. Now, listen, I've locked Karen in the bathroom, I don't want her to know that. I'm going back up there. I don't think he'll move. You phone the doctor first and then phone the police. Tell Allsopp it's Niles, the police are probably coming to look for Janice Hedden. If not – well, you phone them after you've spoken to the doctor. I'm going to put Karen in her room, I'll lock her in. Everything will be all right as long as we keep control."

She couldn't believe it. For a moment she stared after him, then she picked up the directory. Her hands were trembling. She found the right page and began to dial. Twice she had to put the receiver down and start again.

"Hullo, Dando two-one-four."

"Is that Mrs Allsopp? It's Louise Magruder. Is your husband in?"

"Who's calling – the line's very bad, you're very faint."

"It's Louise Magruder, from Trencher's Farm. I must speak to Gregory."

"Oh, hullo, Louise. Awful weather, isn't it? I'm afraid Gregory's not here, he had to go to the Hedden place with Mrs Hedden, you heard what happened?"

"I was there. Look, Alice, I don't know –"

"You'll have to speak up, dear, you've gone very faint again."

She couldn't shout, *he* would hear. She made a speaking trumpet with her hands.

"Alice, we ran into a man on the road, with the car. It's Niles."

"What was that? You hit somebody?"

66

"Yes. Henry Niles. Do you understand? Niles, the murderer?"

"What, Henry Niles! Are you sure?"

"George says it's him. Oh my God, I don't know what to do. He's lying on our couch. George says he might be hurt."

"You poor dear! That's terrible. You must phone the police at Compton Wakley. Gosh, they're looking for him on the moor, it's been on the wireless. Oh –"

"What's wrong?"

"Oh God! I've just remembered, they can't get through from Compton Wakley. Somebody phoned them about Janice Hedden. They phoned Gregory and said their cars couldn't even get as far as Fourways Cross. You're not alone, are you?"

"George is here. We don't know what to do with him. Should we give him something – we've only got whisky and gin?"

"Now for goodness sake don't worry. Listen, I'll phone the Inn, Harry Ware can send somebody to the Heddens. They're not on the phone, worse luck. I should phone the police anyway, if I were you, they may try to get through again, they've got snowploughs."

"But what'll we do about *him*? He's just lying there on the couch, he may be dying or *anything*."

"Keep him warm and don't let him move. I wouldn't give him anything to drink, he may have a haemorrhage or something. Look, we'd better ring off. I'll phone the Inn and you phone the police. Gregory will try to get over as soon as he can.'

Louise dialled the operator.

"I want the police at Compton Wakley," she said. "I can't find the number. It's very urgent."

"Their line's been busy," said the male operator. "I'll try them."

She stood by the window-ledge, the receiver pressed hard against her ear, faint voices and crackling on the line. She heard footsteps in the sitting-room.

"George?"

There was no answer.

"George?"

"Connecting you now," said the operator.

"GEORGE!"

"Just a minute, you're not through yet."

"GEORGE!"

The door handle turned. She seemed paralysed. Then George came into the hall.

"I thought it was *him*!"

"You're through now," said the operator. "Go ahead."

"It's the police."

"I'll take it," he said. "You go up and get Karen into bed, here's the key. Try not to let her know you're locking the door. Hullo, is this the police? My name is Magruder, I live at Trencher's Farm near Dando Monachorum – I know the line's bad. Listen, I think we've got Henry Niles here. Henry Niles! Yes, that's right. I'll hold on. The number is Dando six nine four. Yeah, I heard you, I'll hold on."

He nodded for Louise to go upstairs.

"Hullo? Yes, that's right, I'm sure it's Niles, his name's stitched inside his coat. My name is Magruder. Look, is it important? All right, M-A-G-R-U-D-E-R. George. We were driving home from Dando Monachorum – that's right, Dando Monachorum – and we hit this guy on the road, I could hardly see for snow. So we brought him back to the house. Yes, that's right, white shirt, brown coat, all right, jacket, grey trousers. Small sort of guy. No, I didn't look that close at his eyes.... We've phoned for the doctor, I think he's in a state of shock or something. He was nearly frozen to death when we got him back here ... so what do we do with him? Can't you get over here? I've got a small daughter in the house. Don't you have snowploughs or such things?"

He listened impatiently. You could never tell if the police believed you or not. It was very cold in the hall. Then the inspector spoke again.

"Well, I suppose so. He doesn't *look* very dangerous."

The inspector told him that the road from Compton Wakley to Fourways Cross was blocked and a snowplough might take all night to clear it.

"I'll send some men walking," the inspector said. "It's eight miles or thereabouts, I don't know how long it'll take them in this kind of weather. Can you make sure he stays there with you?"

"Yeah, I suppose so. Look, Inspector, I've got a small daughter here, do you think I'm going to push off for a moonlight stroll or something ... yeah, I know all about him. You may think this is funny, but when you people were thinking

68

of hanging him back there I was one of twelve professors who signed a letter to *The London Times*. My wife's English. I know all about him."

"We'll try to get through as quick as we can," said the inspector. "If anything happens – give me a ring."

"Well, yeah, I can do that. What would you do, ask him to come to the phone? All right."

He put down the phone and went into the sitting-room. Niles had not moved. His eyes seemed fixed on one spot on the ceiling. He had a pale, insignificant face and wispy hair. So that was Henry Niles – the monster! A small lump of nothing. Was that the creature whose very name had made parents tremble?

Ten years ago it was, when Niles had become a sort of symbolic figure of his time. He had been caught after he'd murdered two children in Salford, up North, and would have been no more than just another addition to the long list of grisly English murderers (whom, George always noted with surprise, the English regarded almost with affection, provided they were dead) had he not escaped after less than a year. The escape made him truly famous, or infamous – the distinction seemed to have lost importance – for he had been out of the asylum only three hours, during which time he had raped, strangled and mutilated a girl of six.

Brought to trial for this murder, Niles became less a man than a battleground over which the forces of 'progress' and 'retribution' fought another of their grimly impersonal campaigns. The public wanted him put to death. Psychiatrists were found who would say that Niles was, in fact, sane enough to be hung. Those who maintained that he was *still* a mental defective were unpopular. The way George had seen it, the English classed Niles with all the other ogres of the time. To them he was like the Nazis, a malignant excrescence to be quickly destroyed. For a time it had seemed that the counter-argument – that Niles would have been obliterated *by* the Nazis – was too sophisticated an exercise in abstract legalism. But an English jury had once again found him not responsible for his actions.

To George this had been one of the most civilised public actions he had ever known. What had his own country to show in the way of parallels? The refined medieval horror of the Chessman case? The British had not hung Niles, for whom nobody could say a good word except that he was an incurable freak. He had loved Britain for that – it had even influenced his attitude to Louise, perhaps creating something of an inferiority complex on his part.

To look at the man now added nothing nor subtracted anything from those arguments fought so bitterly ten years before. On the couch he was just a funny little man with some kind of nose blockage that made him breathe noisily through his mouth.

How could you think of him as a symbol – or a monster – when you had taken a towel and dried his chilled feet with their curiously misshapen toes?

He sat in an armchair and looked at Niles. The sensation was a kind of electrifying anti-climax. Here he was, Henry Niles, a human agent of all the blind forces of evil that surrounded mankind. Words seemed to mean nothing. What you looked for was some sign.

Bafflingly, there was no sign.

So excited by Mrs. Allsopp's phone call that he didn't stop to think, Harry Ware hurried into the bar and spoke to the nearest men. The bar was crowded.

"Here, Niles is at Trencher's Farm," Harry Ware blurted out. "That American ran into him on the road, knocked him down. They want somebody to get over to the Heddens and fetch the doctor."

Men who had been out in the cold and snow in search parties looking for Janice Hedden pushed towards Harry Ware. Other villagers and farmers were still out searching. In that weather men needed a drink and a warm after an hour tramping through the snow.

"Henry Niles – in Dando?"

Men looked at each other in horror. Janice Hedden was missing and Henry Niles was in Dando.

"What about the girl?" somebody asked.

"They didn't say." Harry Ware looked from face to face. It was as if this was a night when anything could happen. Not since the war had so many Dando men left their homes at the same time. When they'd heard that the road was blocked and the police could not help, they'd formed into parties to comb the village and its surrounds for the missing girl. Something had happened in Dando and nobody would come from the

70

outside to put it right.

"Chris Cawsey's got his Land-Rover, he could get through to the Heddens," said one of the farmers. "Somebody'll need to take the doctor up there."

"Doctor? It ain't a doctor they'm need, not for that devil."

Harry Ware looked round for Chris Cawsey. As far as he could remember Chris had been out most of the evening, with one search party or the other. He'd only recently come back to the Inn.

"Can you get up there in the Land-Rover, Chris?" he asked.

"Can always have a try," said Cawsey. Harry Ware thought at the time there was something strange about Chris. He seemed to be trying to keep a straight face – as though he wanted to giggle. Still, there was no accounting for what happened to people in circumstances like this. Some men bought pints and talked excitedly. Some went out, to pass the news round the search parties.

When he got behind the wheel of the Land-Rover, Chris Cawsey was making little chirping noises to himself. He'd had some real fun that night, not half he hadn't. And maybe there would be more.

As he drove off through the village other men began walking up the long, dark road to Trencher's Farm.

Dando was on its own. The outside world couldn't help. And it couldn't interfere.

CHAPTER SEVEN

"I don't like sitting here – with him," Louise said. "Couldn't we move somewhere else?"

George looked at Niles. With the *Esse* stove turned up the sitting-room had become very warm. He thought Niles' eyelids were beginning to drop.

"I think he's going to sleep," he said. "I don't like the idea of moving him, we don't know what might have been injured –"

"Oh my God, George – it's Niles – you'd think he was some kind of innocent victim."

He looked at his wife in surprise. Louise moved over to the sitting-room window.

71

"Close the curtains, honey," he said. "You can't see anything out there."

"We could put him upstairs in the spare bedroom, it's got a key."

"I said I don't think we should move him."

"For God's sake, George!"

"You don't need to shout. I'm –"

"I'll scream the roof off in a minute! I'm not staying in the room with that man."

George Magruder was not a *real* coward, he was sure of that. The academic, sedentary life didn't give a man much chance to prove himself in physical challenge, but he was sure he could face danger as well as most men. No, it wasn't cowardice that normally let Louise get her own way. He *loved* her. These were modern times, men no longer ruled with an iron hand. They were equals. And there was no point to rows between equals, they were a pointless waste of energy.

"Look, Louise, do you really want him upstairs – with Karen just along the landing?"

Louise shut her eyes, clenching her lower lip between her teeth. Damn George, damn him, always so bloody sensible!

"We could lock him in," she said, less angrily.

"Well I guess we could but he was supposed to be locked up in a lunatic asylum, wasn't he? Maximum security? If he could escape from them I don't imagine any old latch would hold him. Of course, you could sit with Karen and I could stay with him."

"In films they handcuff them to bedposts ... and things. Oh well, let him stay there." They both looked at Niles. His eyes had closed. "I'd better take Karen her hot drink. Thank goodness she had all that cake and stuff at the party, I don't think I could have cooked *anything* tonight."

On her way from the kitchen through the dining-room and then up the stairs she felt ashamed of herself – although this didn't improve her temper. She knew she was behaving badly. She couldn't help it.

Despite the hot-water radiator, Karen's room was cold. She put the tray on the bed and went to the curtains to check that the window hadn't been left open. Down below she saw a patch of light on snow in front of the study window. Wind drove big flakes against the glass. She could hear the movement of the trees across the track.

As she made to pull the curtains her eye seemed to catch a dark movement down below. She put her face close to the pane, but there was nothing to be seen.

"You'd better put a cardigan over your pyjamas," she said to Karen. "Here's some Horlicks – I could warm up a mince pie if you're hungry."

"I'm not hungry. Who is that man downstairs? Why did you and Daddy shout at each other? I feel awful."

"Now now, darling, we were a bit upset, that's all. He's just a man who was out in the snow, he's almost frozen to death, poor chap."

Karen had her father's habit of staring blankly at you, as though you had just told an obvious lie and she was giving you a chance to recant. It was a common characteristic in America. She'd never discovered whether the dead-pan face was meant to express contempt, or was a sign of incomprehension.

"Why are you staring at me like that, Karen?"

"I don't like that man. Why did Daddy lock my door, Mummy?"

"Did he, dear? You probably just imagined it."

"No, I heard him. He locked the door. You unlocked it when you came up."

Louise heard a noise down below – from outside. She stared at the curtains, a Brer Rabbit pattern on yellow. The walls of the room were white. She listened.

"What is it, Mummy?"

"Nothing, dear. You drink your Horlicks before it gets cold." She tried to be casual about walking to the window and lifting the corner of the curtain. Again there was nothing to be seen, just snow cascading through light thrown from the downstairs window. She felt terrified.

"I'll be back up in a minute or two, Karen. You finish your Horlicks."

"But Mother –"

"Do as you're told, Karen."

She tried to turn the key at the same time as she clicked the latch. She put the big key in the pocket of her sheepskin jacket. She walked along the corridor, past the door of their bedroom, past the door of the store-room, past the spare bedroom. The upstairs corridor was just wide enough for one person to walk along with both shoulders almost touching the walls. Off the small, square landing there was the two steps that led to the

73

bathroom and lavatory, and the well of the stairs down to the sitting-room.

Normally, when she went downstairs, she switched off the corridor light. She'd learned to take care of light bulbs. Twice she'd had to drive the eight miles to Compton Wakley when a bulb failed. That was the nearest hardware shop. Her fingers rested on the switch. Then she decided to leave the light on. Somehow it made her feel safer.

"Did you hear something outside, George?"

He was standing by the sitting-room window, his head turning towards her as though she'd caught him doing something secretive.

"Outside? There's nothing outside. On a night like this? It must have been the wind."

"You did hear it then?"

"It was the wind. Calm down, Louise, nothing's going to happen. The police will be here shortly."

"Yes? Walking all the way from Compton Wakley? They might never get here." She didn't like the nasty, brittle tone in her voice, but there was nothing she could do about it. "God, why did *we* have to run into him?"

"Maybe we saved his life. You wouldn't want him out there, would you? He'd freeze to death."

"I wish he bloody had."

"More convenient than hanging him, huh?"

"There isn't any hanging now."

"There was when he –"

Somebody knocked on the front door. A heavy, impatient knock. They looked at each other. Relief came into their faces. George went to the sitting-room door. Louise followed, standing in the entrance to the hall, looking back to make sure Niles was still asleep.

George opened the front door. A cold blast of wind rushed round the hall. It was dark outside. He stepped back to the switch which worked the outside porch light.

Three men stood in the shelter of the porch, bulky figures in heavy coats and rubber boots, caps shading their faces.

"You got Niles here?" said one.

"Yeah. Come in."

George fumbled for the door chain.

"We rang the police," he said, slipping the chain from its

74

slide. "Come in. They said they'll be here as fast as they can make it."

"Us don't want no police," said another man. George didn't pay much attention. The thought of having the responsibility for Niles taken off his shoulders made him excited. He let the first two men go into the sitting-room. The third hung back in the porch.

"Come in, won't you? That's some weather out there."

The man came in. George closed the front door. It took a few seconds for the three men to get into the sitting-room, their bulk jamming in the narrow doorway. When they saw Louise they took off their caps. George recognised two of them. They'd been in the bar that night he'd gone down to the Inn. A very big man with a red face and a younger guy with dark hair and long sideboards. He didn't know if he'd seen the third man before or not. A shifty sort of man with a weaselly face.

"That's him," he said, pointing to Niles, who was still asleep. "We hit him in the snow, I was on him before I could see him."

The men looked like farm-workers. The one with the sideboards looked at Niles and said something to the other two, George didn't catch what he said, the local dialect was beyond him. He could smell liquor.

"You haven't brought the doctor, have you?" he asked, uncertainly. "I think we might have injured him –"

"Not bloody hard enough," said the young man. Norman Scutt had been over-awed for a moment or two, in the strange room, with the woman there. "What's he done with Janice Hedden, that's what us want to know."

Suddenly he went past Louise and bent over Niles, shoving his fingers into the sleeping man's chest. "Wake up, Niles, what've you done wi' Janice Hedden then? Don't kid on you're sleeping."

"Hey, don't push him," said George. "He might have a broken rib or something."

"He'll have worse if he don't tell us where Janice Hedden is. Wake up, you, bloody madman. Where's the little girl?"

Again he shoved hard into Niles' chest. Henry opened his eyes. He made as though to say something, then closed his mouth. He tried to twist over on to his side, drawing his knees up under the blankets. Norman Scutt grabbed his shoulder and pressed him back against the couch.

"Tell us where the girl is, you bloody pervert!"

Henry blinked rapidly.

George frowned. He didn't understand why these men had come.

"Look, don't push him," he said, his voice still polite and reasoning. "If he's got a broken rib you could push it into his lungs. Are you one of the search parties? Look, I don't think he could have had anything to do with Janice Hedden, he was pretty well helpless when we found him, he was walking down the hill, she couldn't have run all the way –"

"He got her, course he did," said Norman Scutt. "Who else'd do it? He's a bloody child murderer, where is she you –"

He raised his right arm as though to punch Niles on the face. George felt he had to do something. Janice Hedden was their business, but he had a responsibility for Niles. He went over to the couch, catching Norman Scutt's raised arm.

"Look, friend, I know you're worried, but –"

"Let goa me, you ain't got nothing to do wi' it."

Norman Scutt tried to shrug his arm free. George tightened his grip. Norman straightened up. They were face to face, George the taller. "You can't *hit* him," George said, frowning. "I'm as worried about the girl as you are but –"

"Oh yeah? You're worried, are you? Then what if she's lying out in the snow? You don't want him to tell us where? Maybe he didn't get time to do her in, maybe he just did his bloody tricks on her –"

"I'm telling you, we met him about a mile and a half up the road from the school. She'd only just run away. He was in a bad way then. How could he have done anything to her?"

Norman Scutt didn't like to hear these things. It was obvious, Niles *must* have got her. Where was she otherwise? He didn't like the yank holding him. He looked at Phillip Riddaway. Big Phil could take care of the yank. He looked at Louise.

George stood between Norman Scutt and the couch. He tried to remember what he'd been taught about unarmed combat in the army, during advanced training, before he'd become an education officer. He recalled vague fragments – hands smashing into throats, fingers going for eyes. He hadn't taken it very seriously then. None of it was appropriate now. He felt embarrassed more than anything else.

"Look, I don't think your friend should stay in the room with Niles," he said to the two other men. Phil Riddaway stared back. Norman had said they'd force Niles to tell them about Janice. Norman hadn't said there would be trouble. Phil didn't know what to think.

The third man – Bert Voizey – never felt comfortable in this kind of fancy house. Like one of his own ferrets, he had a natural instinct for creeping about in darker corners. He was not at ease with loud, confident people who stared you straight in the eye when they talked to you.

"You'd better calm down like, Norman," he said, smirking apologetically at Louise.

"Us come here to get that bloody pervert," said Norman.

Louise took it for granted that there was nothing to fear from three local men, however angry they were. In fact, she was just a little bit pleased to see a man ruffle George's pomposity. She wondered what he would do.

"Well nobody's getting him," said George. "Look, if it makes you any happier I'll ask him. I don't believe he's capable of speaking." He went over to the couch. "Hey, you awake, Niles?"

Henry seemed to cower, his eyes blinking even more rapidly than before.

"Nobody's going to hurt you. Did you see a little girl tonight? Before the car hit you?"

Henry opened his mouth several times. He was still shivering, although it was very warm in the sitting-room and he must have been even warmer under the thick blankets.

"Come on, try and tell us, did you meet a little girl? A *girl*?"

Henry seemed to shake his head. Then tears came into his big, wide eyes. George felt embarrassed. He turned to the three men.

"You see? He's just a helpless mess. I think you guys would be better employed looking for Janice instead of standing here. I'd go with you but I'm not leaving him here with my wife."

"No, you wouldn't," said Norman Scutt. "That's different, ain't it, *your* kid."

Unsure as he was in dealing with these strangely spoken Englishmen, George resented the imputation.

"I said to the police I'd keep him right here till they arrive," he said. "They made me responsible for him."

"Come on, Norman, us are supposed to be doin' a search," said Bert Voizey.

With another two drinks in him Norman would have refused to go, but he was just on the right side of caution. A
well-lit sitting-room, with a respectable woman present, wasn't
the kind of place you could start trouble. Not unless you had
a good excuse. And the bloody American hadn't given him an
excuse. Phil Riddaway was used to obeying men who spoke
with authority.

Grumbling, Norman Scutt allowed himself to be shown to
the door.

"If he says anything I'll let you know," George said, holding
the front door open. They crowded into the porch. "Honestly,
I don't think he could've done anything to her."

"Bugger you an' what you think," Norman snarled, but
Bert Voizey pulled him away. Phillip followed, not sure what
he was expected to do.

"I hope you find her," George shouted, but they were already moving off into the blizzard. He shut the door.

"God, you really excelled yourself there," said Louise. "Did
it make you feel like a hero, protecting that poor innocent
man? I'd have let them tear him from limb to limb if there was
the slightest chance he knew where she was."

"Don't be stupid, Louise. You know as well as I do he
couldn't have."

"I don't know anything. It would be us, wouldn't it? *We've*
got to protect that – that animal."

"Why don't you make some coffee, honey? I know it's been
a helluva thing to happen but –"

When the window smashed they both jerked round. A stone
fell on the floor underneath the curtains.

"Jesus Christ!"

George went to the window and pulled back the curtain.
One of the four panes was punctured by a ragged hole. He
could see nobody outside. He went quickly to the front door,
but Bert Voizey had already pulled Norman Scutt out of sight
down the lane, followed by Phil Riddaway. He locked the door
and slipped the chain into its slide.

"Oh George, I'm scared," said Louise, her hands across her
throat, her forearms covering her breasts as though she were
naked. For a moment he was glad they'd thrown the stone, it
had taken the anger out of Louise.

"Oh don't worry, they're only silly bastards. Still, I suppose you can understand how they feel. We're lucky they went so peacefully."

It had been no easy business to get Mrs. Hedden up the stairs and into bed, with Tom Hedden interfering rather than helping. Doctor Gregory Allsopp waited in the bedroom, which was as dirty and untidy as the rest of the house, until the sedation pills began to take effect. He was tired. His car had stopped in the snow about half a mile from the Hedden farm and he and Tom – who was half-drunk and full of self-pity – had carried her the rest of the way in a fireman's lift, Tom stumbling and cursing, his wife hysterical. Eventually it was Bobby Hedden who had helped him up the stairs with his mother, Tom being at that annoying stage of drink where everything he said and did only added to the general confusion.

If he had not long ago disciplined himself in the ways of these Dando people, Gregory Allsopp would have felt angry at Tom. Mrs. Hedden was anaemic and should have been under treatment for months. Having five children between the ages of fifteen and three, as well as doing the woman's work about the farm, would have been taxing enough for any woman, but add to that her anaemia *and* the strain of looking after Janice and you had one of those cases that made a doctor's logical mind *fume*. But a doctor's logic came from another world. Doctors could see what was wrong with people's lives – but society wasn't interested in doctors' views. It wanted the doctors to patch people up after the damage had been done. Any attempt to prevent the damage was either Utopian nonsense or patronising interference. He talked to Tom Hedden in what he knew were the only terms he'd understand. He made sure Bobby was listening, for it was really up to the boy.

"You must understand what the position will be if she has any more strain," he said. "She may have a breakdown and you'll be on your own for a long time. Do you understand that?"

"Oh aye," said Tom Hedden, "her'll stay in bed. It's not her us are worried about, it's Janice, where is she, what's happened to her?"

"She'll turn up, don't worry," said the doctor. "I'm going back to the Inn, they'll take her there when they find her. She's

79

probably gone to somebody else's house, somebody without a telephone. The important thing is to keep Mrs. Hedden in bed."

Father and son both nodded, but he wondered. People presented one face to a doctor – as they did to a policeman or a priest or a landlord – and kept their real thoughts until they were on their own. He knew well enough what would happen – Mrs. Hedden would wake up in the morning and they'd tell her she was supposed to stay in bed and she'd get up anyway and they would let her. And perhaps she wouldn't have a breakdown this time ... he suppressed a flicker of anger. No doctor could afford to become emotionally involved with his patients' troubles, for there were too many troubles. People like the Heddens could not be helped.

He was about to leave, fastening up his coat for the long walk back to his car, when they heard a motor outside. Gregory Allsopp thought it might be somebody come from the village to help look after the Hedden children. The three younger boys had been fed and put to bed by Bobby, but they were making a lot of noise.

It was Chris Cawsey who came out of the snow that blew round the yard. Gregory Allsopp saw people not as farmers or mechanics but in the light of what he knew of their medical history. He hadn't treated Cawsey since he'd left school yet from what he had heard and seen he had always felt there was something not quite right about Chris Cawsey. As a boy the kind of trouble he'd got into was not the ordinary sort of trouble boys get into.

"Here, Dr. Allsopp, they'm got Henry Niles up at Trencher's Farm," Cawsey blurted out before he was actually inside the house. "They'm want you up there, that yankee fella run him down on the road."

"Niles?" said Tom Hedden, his brain and his voice thick with drink. "Niles the looney?"

"Yeah. The doctor's wife phoned the Inn, like, Harry Ware asked me to come up here and fetch the doctor."

"Can you get up that road?" Gregory Allsopp asked. Even as he tried to think of what he'd have to deal with at Trencher's he was subconsciously noting something peculiar about Chris Cawsey. He was excited, but there seemed to be more to it than the news of Niles.

"I reckon so."

80

"You can drive me up there then," he said. "Did they say how badly hurt he was?"

"I dunno."

Tom Hedden seemed to be hit by a sudden idea. He turned without speaking and left the kitchen.

"Remember, Bobby," said Gregory Allsopp, "keep your mother in bed, you'd better stay with her, your father seems a bit upset."

"He's pissed drunk," said Bobby.

"And I should try and quieten the other boys, they sound as if they're fighting."

"Always are," said Bobby.

"I'll be back tomorrow."

He was following Chris Cawsey across the yard, the beam of his heavy torch giving little light in the heavy, slanting snow, when Tom Hedden came floundering up behind them.

"You stay at home, man," said Gregory Allsopp. "Look after your kids."

"They'll be all right," said Hedden, walking on. "If they'm got that looney bugger kids'll be all right."

It was then Gregory Allsopp noticed that Tom Hedden was carrying something. A stick, he thought. He lifted the torch. Cradled in his right arm Tom Hedden was carrying a shotgun.

"Hey, Tom, what's that you've got?"

"Where's the Land-Rover, Chris?" Hedden shouted.

"Up past the barn, couldn't risk bringin' her down the hill."

"Tom!" Gregory Allsopp had to run to catch up with Hedden. He grabbed at the sleeve of his black donkey-jacket. "What are you carrying that gun for?"

"That's for him, Niles!"

"What do you mean? Are you bloody mad, man? Get back inside, you're drunk."

"That's what happened to my Janice. That looney got her. Well I'll get him."

"You certainly will not."

Hedden ignored him.

"He's got a shot-gun, Chris," he shouted ahead. Cawsey made no reply. They were on the short slope up past the barn. Gregory Allsopp knew Tom had been drinking at lunchtime and then again at night. There was no knowing what he would

81

do with the gun if he got near Niles. Allsopp ran forward, grabbing the barrel of the shotgun.

"Give that to me, Tom."

"I need it for him. That's who had our Janice, that Niles."

"I said give me that."

They swayed as the doctor tried to pull the shotgun out of Tom Hedden's hands.

"Help me, Chris," he called, but again there was no answer. The torch fell into the snow, its beam diffusing into a soft glow. The doctor slipped. Tom Hedden pushed his face and jerked the gun free. The doctor grabbed at Tom Hedden's knees. The farmer tried to pull himself away but the doctor held on. Tom Hedden jabbed the butt of the shotgun into the doctor's face.

"What the hell –"

He grabbed at the butt, but this time Tom Hedden swung hard. The stock crashed down on the doctor's head. Gregory Allsopp went down face first.

"Let me alone," Tom Hedden shouted. He raised the shotgun again and stabbed the butt down. Then he turned to Chris Cawsey, the gun raised ready to strike again. "I'm goin' up there to that Niles," he said. "You goin' wi' me?"

"Come on." Chris Cawsey giggled. "You'm hit the doctor then," he said. "Hit him real hard like."

"I don't want no interferin'."

They got into the Land-Rover. Snowflakes began to stick to Gregory Allsopp's hair like metal filings to a magnet. . . .

The wind cut into their faces and hard-driven snow was blinding them, but the three policemen, Sergeant Wills and Constables Picken and Davies, pushed on as fast as they were able to plunge through the drifts. Their three torches made little impression on curtains of snow. When they spoke they had to shout at each other's ears, so loud was the howl of the wind.

"We still on the bloody road?" yelled Davies.

"Look out for the big oak," Wills yelled back. The big oak stood on the road to Fourways Cross, just before it sloped down between high banks to Drabble Ford. He estimated they had come a mile. It was two and a half miles from the main road at Compton Wakley to Fourways Cross, where roads led to Compton Fitzpaine, South Compton, Beal Bishop and

Dando Monachorum. From the cross it was four miles to Dando and then they had about two miles to the farm where Niles was.

Before they reached the oak tree they had been off the road twice, the wind-packed drifts having reached the level of low banking.

On the down slope to Drabble Ford they made no faster time, for between the high banks the drifts were deeper, sometimes waist-high. They were slowed up again when they came to Drabble Ford and found it flooded up on to the road on either side. They waded gingerly across the dark rush of water, hand in hand, icy water pouring over the tops of their thigh-length rubbers. Sergeant Wills looked at his watch, holding his torch across his chest. It had taken them just under an hour to come a mile and a half.

"We'd been better off in the bloody Canadian mounties," shouted Davies.

"Keep going, lads," said Wills. "God knows what them Dando buggers'll be getting up to."

He decided that they would have every reason for stopping at the first farm they came to. It wasn't the first time men had died of cold and exposure in weather like this. At least they could be sure Henry Niles wouldn't be travelling far. . . .

"Us'll have to walk her," said Chris Cawsey. "She won't go up the hill."

"I'd walk a hundred miles for that bugger," said Tom Hedden. They got out of the Land-Rover and started up the hill on the road from Dando Monachorum to Trencher's Farm. On the way up they met Voizey and Norman Scutt and Phil Riddaway.

"They'm got Niles up there?" asked Hedden.

"Yeah, an' I'd have got from him where your Janice is but for that yank," said Norman Scutt. "Still, I had a stone into his window, bigmouth bugger."

"Tom's got a gun for Niles," said Chris Cawsey, giggling again. "That right, Tom, you'm goin' to show him?"

"He knows where my Janice is," said Tom Hedden. "A devil like that – with my little girl!"

He started off up the road.

"You comin'?" Chris Cawsey said to the others. "I reckons Tom'll create a bit of havoc."

83

"It ain't right, that pervert," said Phil Riddaway. Norman had told him about perverts. They did terrible things to little girls.

"Come on, then," said Norman Scutt. "We'll show that yank he ain't going to let a bloody kid get murdered just because he thinks he's Mr. Big."

They hurried to catch up with Tom Hedden. Chris Cawsey almost skipped with excitement. He put his right hand under his heavy jacket, pushing his fingers into the warmth of his belly. He felt the hard length of the knife down his thigh. It made him feel like giggling out loud.

Louise Magruder was standing at the *Aga* waiting for the coffee to boil when she heard the noise. She thought it must be George slamming a door. She heard it again. She went through the dining-room into the sitting-room. George was standing in the doorway to the hall.

"What is it?" she asked.

"There's somebody kicking the door," he said.

"Maybe it's the doctor?"

"Does it *sound* like the doctor?"

It sounded like a gang of wild, shouting men trying to batter the door down.

CHAPTER EIGHT

George tried to avoid Louise's eyes. Perhaps she expected him to open the door and throw these men over the garden wall. Perhaps he didn't want her to see that he was frightened. He knew very clearly the difference between a stray brick hurled through a window and the overt hostility of attacking their front door. These men were serious about getting Niles. Something had changed.

"Go away," he shouted.

"I want that Niles," came back Tom Hedden's high-pitched voice.

"You're not getting him, go away."

They went on kicking.

"Don't worry, the door's very solid, it'll stand up to a whole army," he said to Louise.

"Will it? Is that all you're going to do, stand here and let them kick it? For God's sake, George, make them stop it."

"How? Pour boiling oil on them from the bedroom window? Listen, to me, Louise, I know how they feel, I'd be the same way if it was Karen out there. They're not *criminals*. If I open the door they'll probably do something they'd regret tomorrow. They'll get tired of it."

The phone rang.

"Oh thank God," she said. "Maybe it's the police."

He picked it up, standing about three feet from the door.

"Who's this?"

"Hallo, Mr. Magruder? This is Knapman here."

"Hallo."

"Int this snow terrible? I never seen such a bad night of it."

"You're not kidding."

George realised that Knapman probably didn't know they had Niles in the house.

"I'm sorry to bother you and that, but Jean wanted to know about your turkey –"

"Turkey?"

"The one you ordered for Christmas like? Jean thought your wife might want her tonight, get her in the oven maybe."

"I dont think we're too worried about the turkey, Mr Knapman. Right now we've got this man Henry Niles inside the house and a gang of drunks kicking the door down."

He explained about Niles.

"Do you know who 'tis outside?"

"There's a young guy, with sideboards, and a big guy, very big, got a red face. They were in the Inn one night I went down, I don't know their names."

There was a pause.

"Look, Mr. Magruder, I was out looking for Janice, I just came back to make sure Jean and the kids were all right, I'm comin' down that way anyway, I'll bring the turkey. I'll be about ten minutes, I'll talk to them, everybody's a bit jumpy with this Janice going off like that. You know how it is.'

"Yeah, sure, I just wish they'd stop kicking the door. Tell them to go and get drunk somewhere else."

When he rang off the kicking had stopped. He listened. Except for the wind in the trees he could hear nothing. He went into the sitting-room. Niles turned his head, staring at them.

"That was Knapman, he's coming over," he said to Louise, patting her arm. "He'll tell them to push off. I don't think they'd listen to me." He looked at Niles. "Are you hurt anywhere?" he asked, speaking as he would to a deaf man or a foreigner, with exaggerated lip movements.

"That blood wasn't my fault," said Henry, shaking his head. "It wasn't me, promise. Gentle Jesus meek and mild."

George and Louise exchanged horrified looks. Niles began to cry.

"It wasn't my fault, promise!" he sobbed. "It was a game, Mr. Pawson put the belt round me."

"OH MY GOD," Louise shrieked.

"Louise, keep calm for Chrissake."

She screamed, her hands at her lips, her eyes wide with terror. Niles shut his eyes and blubbered like a baby.

At that moment the room was suddenly filled by what seemed like an explosion. The curtains moved as though punched by a giant fist. A brick fell on the stone floor under the window ledge.

He ran to the window. This time they were standing close, faces peering in at him from the darkness, their shadowy silhouettes traced by snowflakes.

"Us want that Niles."

It was a silly thing to say at a moment like this, but it was the first thing that came into his head:

"Get off my land."

"Us'll burn the bloody house down if us don't get him."

"I'll give you one more warning. Go away now and there won't be any trouble. But lift another finger and so help me I'll have you in jail!"

He let the curtain fall back. He had to hope that they'd be shaken by a show of confidence.

"Let them have him, for God's sake!"

"Keep a grip on yourself, honey. Why don't you go upstairs and see to Karen? She'll be terrified at all this noise."

"I don't –"

"Louise! I know this is a hellish situation but *please* don't make it any worse."

She gave him a look of such contempt he thought she was going to spit in his face. Then she went up the stairs.

"That blood wasn't me," Niles groaned, his face red and blotchy with tears.

"Shut up, you," George snarled.

Niles went into a fit of crying. He was so much like a child George almost got down on his knees to comfort him.

Instead he closed the door at the foot of the stairs. The thing was to stay cool. Outside in that weather the drink would soon wear off and they'd go home.

"Mibbe us oughter clear off, Norman," said Bert Voizey. The little rat expert didn't like this kind of business. One thing to get your own back on somebody by slipping poison to his pigs, but not to go fighting like this, face to face.

"Nah, the cops won't be here for hours. I'll smash every window in the bloody house. Us'll get that Niles, I tell you us will. He don't have no right to live, an animal like that. Them coppers get him and what'll they do, eh? Put him back in Two Waters, that's all. An' he killed them kids – and Janice. I'm fed up wi' lettin' them get away wi' it."

"I want that Niles," roared Tom Hedden, who didn't seem to care, or even notice, what the others were doing. "I'll blow his bloody brains out I will!"

Phillip Riddaway kept thinking of what Norman had told him. That Niles was a human devil, he'd got hold of little Janice Hedden and done awful things to her, like them other kids. He was an animal.

In all his life Phillip Riddaway had only once gone farther than fifteen miles from Dando Monachorum, when they'd sent for him to take army tests. He hadn't liked the town, all them people pushing and shoving and staring at him. It had turned out all right, for the army had written to his mother saying they didn't want him. He was forty-seven, stronger than any man in Dando or Compton. Everybody knew that. Norman was always telling him how strong he was. Norman was his special pal. Norman had told him what it was like to do things with a woman. Norman had been in gaol and had travelled to hundreds of different places. Norman said a man had only one or two real pals and he ought to stick by them. In prison, Norman said, the men didn't like these animals who did awful things to little kids. Norman had told him how one of these devils had come to Norman's prison and the men – Norman's prison pals – had got a razor blade and cut chunks out of the bugger's backside. Norman knew a lot about it. Norman said that all them posh people didn't care what happened to folks like them, even little girls. That made him very angry. Just because he didn't have any little girls of his own didn't mean he would let a devil like this Henry Niles do awful things and get away with it. He felt very angry. Norman was right, they ought to burn the house down.

"Us want to get into the house and get Niles without that yank seein' us like," said Bert Voizey.

"Aye, you'm be a bloody burglar, Norman," said Chris Cawsey, "you'm show us how to get into her." He laughed. His hand was resting on his knife. When he pushed the sheath the tip would touch his john thomas. That was good. If he could get in there he'd use his lovely knife. Better than sheep! Nobody knew the kind of high jinks *he* got up to with his lovely knife. He thought of the American man's wife, he'd seen her walking about in the village. She'd have lovely big tits on her. It made him want to laugh out loud, just thinking about them. And the knife. What it would do to them!

"Us goin' round the back," said Norman. "Kick the door, Tom, us'll slip in a window and have that Niles out dead easy."

George Magruder was trying to stick squares of cardboard over the broken panes with Scotch tape when he heard a noise from the kitchen. He knew the back door was locked, but there was a big window in the kitchen. The other windows in the house were fairly small, the panes hardly big enough for a man to crawl through head first, but the kitchen window would be easy to get through. Before he left the sitting-room he looked at Henry Niles, who seemed to have sobbed himself back to sleep. It was hard to realise that all this passion had been aroused by that small, scruffy baby-man. You looked at him sleeping, an ugly little thing of a human being, and you tried to imagine those hands tearing the life out of a child. It made you feel sick.

But that wasn't the point. When they'd hit him he'd been wandering about on the road, half frozen. The girl had only been out of the school fifteen minutes at the most. He couldn't have – unless ... unless she'd run up the hill ... unless Niles was walking *up* the hill when they'd hit him ... how long did it take? He shuddered. If only the damn police were here. If only they weren't stranded in this desolate hole. It was ridiculous to think that in this day and age, in England, a man could find himself under siege by a gang of crazy drunks and have nobody to call on for help. Ridiculous.

88

He heard the noise again. He ducked his head to avoid the beam which straddled the doorway between the small dining-room and the kitchen. Through the kitchen window he saw a man's face and hands. They were trying to force the latch.

He felt angry. And sick. There was something nauseating about people trying to force their way into your house.

"Go away," he shouted.

The man vanished. Through the glass he could see only snowflakes. He checked the window latch. It was that kind with a swan-neck handle and a short, thin bar of metal which slipped upwards into a slot in the centre window post. The two frames moved outwards from the centre post. At the bottom of each frame there was a long metal bar with holes for fitting over a metal peg. Once the glass was broken a man would only have to put his hand inside and both the metal bar and the catch would open in two seconds. He couldn't see a way of securing the catches.

He checked the door which opened into the small kitchen porch. That had a Yale lock and a fairly strong bolt. He didn't think they could force it. The outside porch door was probably unlocked. Still, it wouldn't do them much good to get into the porch.

He went back to the sitting-room. Henry Niles was sitting up, the blankets round his waist.

"I need the lavvy," he said. George wondered what kind of accent Niles had. Not from these parts. Niles had been about twenty-three when they'd caught him that first time. What kind of life had he had before? How long had his warped mind been preparing him for the moment he got his hands on a little girl? Or had he been doing it for a long time before they caught him, gradually working up to a murder? What did it all mean? A man like that, the mind perverted. Child-like, but warped. what did it all *mean*?

"I need the lavvy," Niles said again.

"It's upstairs," George said. "I'll show you."

That was another thing. Although he knew the man was a murderous lunatic he still found himself adhering to the normal rules of politeness. Was he frightened he might hurt Niles' feelings? What could he do, ask the guy what it felt like to be a child-murderer?

This pathetic little man, who could hardly walk by himself to the foot of the stairs, was *he* the symbol of the age, the personification of blind, unthinking evil? The ultimate in perverted lust? How could you say he was perverted when you knew he had the mind of a child? You couldn't punish him – that was what progress and civilisation meant, if it meant anything at all. Yet they'd hung the Nazis. Were they *responsible*? Were they perverted beyond the stage where normal human rules applied?

Perhaps it was too much to ask people to excuse the evil done by Henry Niles. Perhaps it would be better all round to have him extinguished. A hundred million people had been killed this century – by normal men. What was so special about Niles' case? Did it matter? What a pointless exercise in so-called progress it seemed, to make a principle out of this shaking little body, climbing the stairs the way Karen had when she first learned to walk, one step at a time, hand clutching the rail.

He showed Niles into the lavatory, the blanket hanging round his shoulders, like a boy playing Red Indians.

"Can you – will you manage?"

Niles nodded. He let the blanket slide to the floor. George turned his head away, disgusted at having seen Niles like that. It was akin to being on good terms with evil. He bolted the door on the outside. It was only a small bolt, but he didn't think Niles was in any state to force it. He went along the corridor and tapped gently on Karen's door.

"Louise?"

She came out, her face drawn with worry.

"Is she sleeping?"

Louise shook her head.

"Come on, I want to speak to you. Better lock her door."

What did he want to tell her? That he was scared? That he was sorry? Sorry for what? Why did she make him feel guilty –inadequate? Was he inadequate – as simple as that?

"They're still outside," he said. They stood in the darkness of their bedroom. He wanted her to reassure him. What was the point of fighting for principles if you couldn't maintain a relationship with your own wife? Was that why some men threw themselves into such battles – as compensation for personal inadequacies? Did those old pioneers tolerate this kind of disruptive influence from their wives?

"If they want him as badly as this we can't stop them," she
90

said. She sounded *bored*. "They wouldn't hurt him, they only want to know what he did to Janice Hedden—"

"You know as well as I do he couldn't have been anywhere near Janice Hedden. So do they. They're all steamed up, you can see that as well as I can. That young one who tried to hit him — do you think he cares a nickelsworth about Janice? The hell he does! They want blood, that's all."

"What does it matter?"

"Don't you *care*?"

"No. Why did it have to be us, that's all I care about. Oh my God, my head's splitting."

"You'd better lie down for a bit."

"With all this going on, silly idiots playing Cowboys and Indians? That's all it is. Stupidity."

Downstairs there was another explosion, glass breaking with a popping noise, the sound a bottle makes when smashed against a brick wall. She drew a deep breath. She thought she was going to vomit.

"Oh let them in! Christ Almighty, George, you know that noise goes right into my nerves."

"Is that all it means to you? I'd better go downstairs."

He was half-way down the stairs when he remembered Niles. He ran back up.

"Louise! Niles is in the john. Stay with Karen."

"Don't leave him up here!"

"Just stay with Karen, damn you."

He ran down the stairs. The noise seemed to have come from the study. He went through the hall. When he opened the study door the room was completely black except for a faint light at the window, where a white gauze curtain blew out in ghostly folds. He felt along the wall for the light switch.

A man's arm was pushed through the pane of broken glass, a hand twisting for the window catch. He felt a wave of revulsion. He had to force himself to go up to the window. He stared at the motionless hand, wanting to hit it, nauseated at its proximity. On the window-ledge there was no possible weapon, only his notes for Branksheer.

"What's wrong with you people?" he shouted. "We've got the police coming. Why don't you go away?"

The hand pulled back through the jagged hole. He couldn't see if the man had run away or was standing outside in the darkness.

Then he heard a voice. Somebody was shouting. Above the wind the words were only noises.

For the first time he began to feel real fear. If more of them had arrived – suppose they'd found Janice murdered? The villagers might come in force, a lynch party. From what he'd seen of Dando folk they were capable of anything. Mysterious people.

Somebody knocked at the door. He went into the hall.

"Go away," he said, lacking the energy to shout. He felt weary.

"It's me," said a muffled voice.

"Yeah. Who're you?"

"Bill Knapman."

"Oh. Just a minute." He opened the door with the chain still in its catch. He saw that it was Knapman. "Come in."

He chained and bolted the door again.

"You got through the enemy lines okay then?" he said. "Come into the sitting-room. Maybe they've run out of rocks."

"I told them to clear off. Tom Hedden's out there, Norman Scutt and Phil Riddaway. Been drinking. Reckon Tom's fair gone crazy with this business."

He didn't say anything about the shotgun. There was no point in telling the American, Tom might get in trouble just for carrying the gun. Bill Knapman was sure they would go away now that he was on the scene.

"The wife sent this down," he said, bringing the turkey out from under his coat, holding it by the neck. George Magruder laughed.

"Where's Niles then?" Knapman asked.

"He's upstairs attending to the call of nature. As a famous maniac he's a disappointment in the flesh – about the size of that bird and not as healthy looking. Come on up and have a look at him. Boy, am I glad you're here. Those guys had us worried. They've heaved three rocks already."

He slipped the bolt on the lavatory door. Niles was still on the lavatory seat, his underpants round his ankles, the blanket round his shoulders.

"I've got the runs," he said, looking up at them, more than ever like a pathetic child. "It wasn't my fault."

Bill Knapman shook his head. George saw Niles staring, then he realised it was the turkey. It would be easy, for a man

92

like Knapman, to break Niles' neck. Get it all over with. Like spearing a boil.

"Shout when you're finished," he said.

"I'm cold," said Niles.

"Yeah, well don't sit there all night."

He closed the door.

"Not much to look at, is he?" said Knapman, shaking his head. "Why they don't hang them buggers I'll never know. What good is he to anybody? Better off dead I reckon."

They went along to the bedroom. George was glad in more ways than one that Knapman had arrived. Maybe his presence would cheer Louise up.

"You go on downstairs, I'll just see to Karen," he said.

She had her head almost under the blankets but her eyes were wide open.

"It's all right, honey, they've gone away now," he said. "Why don't you go to sleep? We'll take care of everything. You weren't scared, were you?"

"I *hate* it here."

"So do I, honey. We'll see about going home, first thing. But it's all right for tonight. Give Daddy a goodnight kiss. Sleep tight, old bean, chin up and all that, eh?"

She managed a little smile.

"Good job I brought something along, like," said Chris Cawsey, taking a full bottle of rum out of his big outside pocket. He pulled the cork and took a pull. He touched Tom Hedden's arm with the bottle. Tom Hedden had a pull.

"Bugger Bill Knapman," he said. They were standing in the shelter of the old shed across the road from the farmhouse. Bert Voizey had pulled Tom in there before he could start anything with Bill Knapman. "It's my Janice he took, weren't it? What's bloody Knapman stickin' his nose in for?"

"He's a knowall that Knapman," said Norman Scutt. "Thinks he can push people about."

"That Niles is an animal," said Tom Hedden. "He's goin' to pay for my Janice."

"Too bloody right, Tom. He's goin' to pay this time. They won't let him get away with it again, dirty murderin' pig!"

They stood together watching the front of the house, the rum bottle passing round. All of them thought of different things, yet they were all there for the same reasons. They were

93

the men nobody took notice of. They were the men who'd never had any luck. All their lives other people had told them what to do, had insulted them, put them in gaol, sneered at them, kept them poor. All the years of resentment were now at flash point. They had the best reason in the world, the one reason that could bring them together, out in the open, face to face with an enemy. Tom Hedden's chest heaved with anger. Bill Knapman had told him to clear off, as though he was a village kid, a nobody. What had happened to his Janice didn't matter, oh no, that Niles could come here and murder his daughter and *they* didn't care, just old Tom Hedden's girl, not right in the head anyway. Oh no, they didn't care. It wasn't their daughters that had been took, only a Hedden brat.

Norman Scutt, the burglar and petty thief, had come there because Niles took him back to a world where he was somebody, the world of prison. Men like Niles were the lowest of the low. He made a thief feel like a judge. Norman Scutt had slept in the same bed with three younger brothers until he was sixteen – when he'd first been sent to a Borstal. Norman Scutt liked to burgle houses. Being in a well-furnished room with a big bed and thick carpets and women's stuff on a dressing-table gave him erections. He lusted to be in houses like that. He hated the people who lived in them, because he couldn't understand why they lived in posh bedrooms and he'd slept with three young brothers. He liked to chuck their drawers on the floor, to stub fag ends out on their swanky carpets – best of all, to make a mess on their carpets, right where it would hit them in the face.

Chris Cawsey liked to touch his own body with the knife. It made him giggle and then pant with excitement. He liked to cut into things. Cats as a boy, kittens, hens ... then sheep. Now he felt like giggling. To do it in a gang, that was better than dodging about in fields on his own. He'd already had a bit of fun that night, just enough to give him the taste.

Bert Voizey liked to poison rats because it made him the man who poisoned rats. People knew him as the rat man, people didn't like rats, they were frightened of rats. They looked at him in a funny way because he knew all about rats. It wasn't often he did things with other people. Other people didn't like him. Now he was with mates, they liked him.

Phillip Riddaway just liked being with Norman. Norman was his pal. Norman didn't laugh at him.

"I want that Niles," said Tom Hedden. "I don't care what that Knapman says, I'm goin' to get that Niles."

"Wait till Bill pushes off, Tom," said Norman.

"No, bugger him, I'm after that Niles."

Tom Hedden left the shelter of the old shed and started across the lane, a strong, thickset man, a jerkiness about his walk, half-drunk, his feet stumbling through the snow.

"GIVE ME THAT NILES," he roared at the curtained windows of the farmhouse. "HE DONE IN MY JANICE."

Bill Knapman was about to leave when they heard the shouts. He looked through the curtains.

"It's Tom Hedden, I'd better go out and speak to him," he said to the Magruders. He could see they were frightened. He felt very confident. These people were outsiders, they didn't know the Dando folk. In the absence of police – or any other authority – it was up to somebody like him to take a lead. "Don't worry about old Tom, he's just over-wrought, that's all. I know him, he'll do what I tell him."

George Magruder took a look through the curtains.

"Is that a gun of some kind he's carrying?" he asked.

"No, I don't think old Tom would have a gun," Knapman said, smiling at Louise. "They're a bit crazy at times round here but they aren't that bad."

"Do you think you should go out?" said Louise.

"I'm not worried about Tom Hedden," said Knapman.

George felt secure. Knapman was a local, he knew all these people, he spoke their language.

In the shed across the road the other men had a last swig of rum and then they came out across the lane, to see what was going to happen.

"I'll shoot the door down if I don't get that Niles," Tom Hedden shouted.

CHAPTER NINE

Before Bill Knapman went outside he told George to put on the porch light.

"Just to let Tom see who it is," he said, smiling again at Louise. "Wouldn't want him thinking I'm Henry Niles or nothing. You'd better stay inside, they know me."

95

He opened the door and stepped out in the open-fronted porch.

"Hullo then, Tom," he called. "What's all this then, out lookin' for rabbits on a night like this?"

"I'm lookin' for Niles."

"Now now, Tom, us don't want no trouble here like, do us?"

Bill Knapman walked out into the garden. He was still smiling.

"You'm bein' a bit stupid ain't you, Tom? What's all this chuckin' bricks through these folks' windows, eh? You'm ought to have more sense, man."

Tom Hedden had heard that voice all his life. Big farmers telling him he didn't ought to drink so much, bank managers telling him he couldn't borrow money, landlords telling him he'd had enough to drink, agricultural inspectors telling him he wasn't farming right, always the same voice saying the same things, come off it, Tom Hedden, stop drinking, Tom Hedden, give up your farm, Tom Hedden, pity about your little girl, Tom Hedden, can't do nothing for your little girl, Tom Hedden, put her in a home, Tom Hedden, we can't take her in a home, Tom Hedden, change your ways, Tom Hedden, treat your wife right, Tom Hedden, work harder, Tom Hedden, go into a factory, Tom Hedden, right from the start, the same men with bigger farms, with more money, looking down on him, making jokes at him, always the same thing, having to borrow from those men, having to be polite, to hold his cap in his hand.

He raised the shotgun till its double barrels pointed just above Bill Knapman's head.

"You tell'm I want that Niles," he said. "You'm tell'm, Bill Knapman, or I'll come in an' get'm."

"Don't be so bloody stupid."

Bill Knapman walked towards Tom Hedden. Snowflakes hit his cheeks.

Tom Hedden thought of all the times he'd heard Bill Knapman talk to him like that. All right for him, he'd started off all right. *He* didn't have bad land. *He* didn't have a poor little girl who wasn't right. Oh no, not Bill Bloody Knapman, he was one of them, friends with the Colonel and the vicar and all that sort. Oh yeah, and friends with that bloody yank. Him that was protecting the murdering devil Niles.

There's a good chap, Tom Hedden. No more of your fool-ishness, Tom Hedden.

"Come on, Tom, you bugger, give us that bloody gun and stop all this nonsense!"

"Nonsense! What about my Janice then? It weren't one of your'n, Bill Knapman! No, it were my Janice. Her never had a chance, from the day her were born. He come here and did it to my Janice. I'm goin' to kill him!"

Bill Knapman saw the others coming up behind Tom Hedden.

"Hey, you lot, Norman Scutt! You get hold of Tom and get him out of here. There won't be nothin' said if he goes now."

"What's it got to do wi' you then?" Norman Scutt shouted back. "You'm think you're the bloody police or somethin'?"

"You'll know all about the police if you don't clear out of here," Bill Knapman replied, angry now. This riff-raff needed to be shouted at. He'd been faced with this kind of thing years ago in the Military Police. He knew how to deal with it. Sharp-ish.

"I want that gun, Tom, you're too drunk to know what you're doing." He walked forward. "And you lot bugger off, bloody trouble-makers."

"That madman killed his Janice," Norman Scutt shouted back. "If he didn't kill her he knows where her is."

"Shut up, Scutt!"

He went at Tom Hedden, walking fast, hands out for the gun.

"Leave me alone," Tom Hedden said, his voice low with bitterness and hate.

Bill Knapman got his hands on the barrel. He tried to pull it out of Hedden's hands.

Phillip Riddaway had listened to everything. Most of all he'd listened to Norman. He jumped to help Tom Hedden. Bill Knapman had hold of the barrels of the shotgun. He and Tom Hedden swayed as they pulled in opposite directions. Phillip Riddaway tried to push Bill Knapman in the chest. The other three moved closer.

George Magruder saw them from the front door, dark fig-ures locked in a slow moving dance. Should he go out? Would that make it worse?

Boom!

One of the figures jumped backwards as though jerked by a

string. For a few moments it tottered on its heels and then went down, backwards. It threshed about for a few, never-ending moments. Then it lay still, a dark hole in the snow.

The other figures stood still. George Magruder gripped his upper lip between finger and thumb until the pain made him wince.

They'd shot Bill Knapman!

"You dirty bastards," he shouted, moving out of the door-way into the porch. They looked at him. "You dirty murdering bastards!"

"Here, he's hardly got no head left at all," Chris Cawsey exclaimed, bending over Bill Knapman's body. "You'm done for him proper, Tom."

Phillip Riddaway couldn't understand it.

"You didn't want to kill nobody," he said, his great face in a frown.

"You guys will pay for this!" George Magruder shouted.

"Shut up and give me that Niles," Tom Hedden shouted back.

Bert Voizey wanted to run and hide.

"We'm better off out of here, Norman," he said. "I didn't reckon on murderin' nobody."

"That's too bad for us is all in it now."

"I never killed nobody!"

"Tell that to the coppers. It's the law. It don't matter who done it, us is all in it together. We all get the same blame, equal."

"What'll us do, Norman?" Phil Riddaway asked. He sounded plaintive.

Norman Scutt knew he was the leader. He had the brains. He knew the law. They'd all get done now for manslaughter. At the very least. There was nowhere they could hide, the Yank knew their faces.

"I'm buggered if I'm goin' to gaol for that devil Niles!" He knew what their only hope was.

They all thought of prison. It was the most terrifying thing they could imagine. They were trapped.

"You'm killed one," said Norman Scutt. "Another won't make no difference. Nobody but him and his wife knows it was us. I don't want to be in gaol till I'm an old man."

Chris Cawsey giggled. Ever since he'd been a boy he'd wan-

98

ted to see what people looked like when they were dead.

George Magruder couldn't move. At the back of his mouth he was choking. His insides had gone all cold. His jaw hung slack. He could feel a heavy pulse beat hammering in his brain. His eyes saw the four men standing in the snow, but his brain stood still. It was as if a flash bulb had gone off in darkness, a brilliant moment of blinding light.

Had he seen Bill Knapman catapult to the ground? Was that Knapman, that dark shape in the snow? Who were these men? *Why?*

"I want that Niles, do you hear me?"

He saw the man with the gun come forward. Still he couldn't move. His tongue seemed to swell and fill his mouth. His throat heaved. A thick spurt of vomit sprung from his stomach and poured out of his mouth. He gasped for breath.

"I WANT THAT HENRY NILES!"

He shuddered. The sight of death, real death, had shocked his whole body. There was nothing he could do. They moved towards him.

"George!"

Louise's scream cut into the paralysis which had blanketed his brain.

He turned and grabbed for the door. He slammed the door shut and fumbled for the chain. His fingers couldn't make the catch fit into its slide. Leaning his whole weight against the door he fought to get the brass fitting into its hole. Then it was home. The door was held by a Yale lock and a heavy latch and the chain.

As they started kicking it, he grabbed Louise's elbow and pushed her into the sitting-room.

"Quick, the light," he said. She didn't move. He banged against her as he jumped for the light switch. Then they stood in the red glow of the *Esse*, listening to the din of the men at the door.

"They shot Knapman," he said to her, whispering. "A shotgun. If it's dark they can't see us. Get upstairs."

"Oh my God, what's going to happen to us?"

"HENRY NILES!"

"They can't get in the door," he said. "They'll try the windows. You get upstairs. I'll –"

Something heavy crashed against the front door. He pulled

99

her away from the sitting-room door.

"Snap out of it, Louise, those men are serious! They'll do anything to get Niles."

"They'll kill us! Let them have Niles! They'll kill us!"

"No! Get upstairs before I hit you, Louise."

"You wouldn't –"

"Get upstairs, you stupid bitch!"

His fingers sank into the firm flesh of her upper arm. He forced her across the darkened room and gave her a shove. She stumbled on the first stair. He slammed the door behind her.

Then he moved along the wall to the window. Keeping his body against the side wall he reached his arm across and pulled the curtains open. With the room in darkness he could see them outside but he didn't think they'd be able to see him. The sitting-room window had four panes, possibly just big enough for a man to squeeze through – unless they got an axe and smashed away the wooden framework.

Where else was there? He had a flashing image of women loading rifles, of men crouching beneath small windows in log walls, of Indians ...

"Look, George, this is madness!" She was back in the sitting-room, her panic seemingly gone. "If you think I'm going to stay in here and let these men smash the windows in – Karen's scared to death. I want you to shove Niles out of the door. Let them do what they want to him!"

Why save Niles? It would be easy, open the door six inches and shove him out in the snow. Let them kill him if they were that crazy. They'd go away. Who cared whether Niles lived or died? What was his life compared to theirs?

"No," he said. "They'll kill him."

"I don't care."

"I do. We'd just be buying peace for ourselves. Look, it won't be that bad. I can keep them out of the house. They'll go away. Bill Knapman was an accident. I don't think they meant to kill him."

"How can you keep them out? They've got a gun, haven't they? I'm telling you to get Niles out of this house, George, right now. If you don't I will."

That would be even easier. Let Louise give them Niles. Nobody would blame him. He could say he was fighting them off in another room. Nobody would blame them.

"No! We said hanging Niles would be a crime, didn't we?"

"That was just *talk*."

"Maybe it was. It's real now. We just give up – the first time anything real happens?"

"Don't be silly. This isn't a bloody film!"

They hammered on the door again.

He felt angry. Who did they think they were, crashing into his *home*?

"We give them Niles now, they'll kill him. We hold on for a little while and the police will be here. It'll all be forgotten. You want to give up that easy?"

They heard something in the kitchen. He ran to the dining-room door. To reach the light switch he crouched, moving across the room in the shelter of the table. He switched off the light. He tried to remember where the light switch was in the kitchen. It had been an ordinary house before this, a house he hadn't even liked very much. Now it was their refuge. It suddenly seemed very important to keep them out. Niles was only part of it. They'd lived in these rooms and now a pack of wild men wanted to break in. They were not going to, not if he could keep them out. It was as simple as that. If you let men smash their way into your *home* you were a nothing.

Where was the switch? The kitchen curtains were still drawn, stiffish bamboo slats on a brass rail. Standing against the wall he peered round the corner of the kitchen door. The switch was about four feet along the wall.

Above the *Aga* cooker, hanging on a hook in the wall recess, he saw the thin poker he used each morning to rake ashes from the bottom of the fire. His hands needed something like that.

There was a scraping noise behind the curtains. They were trying to force the catch again.

He had to take a chance that the man at the big window wasn't the one with the shotgun. Treading softly on linoleum, he moved round the corner of the wall and reached his left hand for the switch. When the light went out the noise stopped. He moved quietly to the cooker and felt for the poker. Then he groped his way along the sink until he was beside the window. Was it better to have the curtains closed or open? Open, with the lights off. He could make out their shapes but to them the room would be in pitch darkness.

He eased the bamboo curtain along its rail, holding himself

tightly against the wall. He saw somebody on the other side of the glass. The stainless steel poker felt very light. He tried to imagine what it would be like to hit a man with it.

He didn't want to hit anybody. If he could make the windows secure they'd probably get tired and go away. Right now, when they were at their craziest, was the vital time. He wondered how he could secure the two window catches. If the catches could be tied together across the post neither half of the window could be opened without smashing the glass. And that noise would give him time to stop them.

Taking a chance that it wasn't the man with the gun, he went to the window and rapped the glass with his knuckles. He thought he saw the figure move away. He went back through the dining-room.

"Louise?"

"Where *are* you?"

She sounded very angry. Whenever she spoke he felt foolish, as though she thought he was playing some kid's game. He moved across the sitting-room.

"Louise?"

Then he saw her, a darker shape against the faint whiteness of the wall. That gave him an idea. If they switched on the upstairs lights, all of them, they'd throw a good light down on the ground all round the house. That way he could see them but they wouldn't be able to see him.

"Listen," he said, standing beside her, "you go upstairs and switch on all the lights, bathroom, lavatory – Christ! Niles! Is he still in there?"

"Karen!"

They bumped into an armchair as they crossed the sitting-room floor. He ran up the stairs. The lavatory door was still bolted.

"You still in there?"

"I'm cold," Niles said, a whine in his voice.

"You'll be colder if you come out."

He went into the bathroom and switched on the light. Normally they didn't bother to pull any of the upstairs curtains. What was the point when your nearest neighbour was a mile away?

"Have we any kind of rope?" he asked Louise.

"Rope! Are you going mad?"

He stared at her, their faces only a foot apart. He felt a

102

wave of rage coming over him. This wasn't how those wives behaved, those pioneering women. They stood by their men, through thick and thin.

"I'll show you who's mad," he said, his mouth tight with anger. He grabbed her by the shoulder, consciously digging his fingers into the bone, hoping it would hurt. "Come here to the window, come on, these are your friends, stand at the window. See anybody? See the guy with the gun? Open the window and shout to him, go on, you think it's just a game. See what he does."

She tried to pull back. He held her close to the window.

"What's wrong, Louise, not frightened, are you? They wouldn't shoot at you, would they?"

"Of course they wouldn't..." but still she pulled to free herself and move away from the window.

"If we can keep them out they'll go away," he said. "They've worked themselves up, that's what it is. Drink and hysteria. You saw what happened to Knapman, for Chrissake. He got killed trying to talk to them."

"It must have been an accident. You said it was an accident."

"Yeah, well we don't want any more accidents. Is there any rope, I want to tie up the window catches."

"I don't know."

"Think!"

"There was a washing line, it was somewhere," she said. "Where?"

"Oh I can't remember now, it was just a washing line!"

"Think! It'll make all the difference."

"It might be in the kitchen, I had it before the snow, I can't remember where I put it –"

This time the noise came from the other end of the house.

"The study," he said.

Glass broke. At the same time there was more kicking at the front door. He went down the stairs two at a time, the thin poker in his right hand. The study door had an old-fashioned latch. As he flicked it up with his thumb he wondered how long it would hold out against a man's weight. Not long. In the darkness of the room the curtain still blew in long, billowing folds, like a woman's diaphanous scarf.

A man's head was inside the broken window, an arm trying to twist round so that a hand could reach the catch. The break-

103

ing glass they'd heard was the man clearing the jagged pieces from the framework.

"Get out of my house," he snarled at the man's head. The arm stopped moving. George knew he had all the advantages. The man was helpless, his shoulder and neck pressed tightly through a collar of broken glass.

It would be easy to grab his collar, pull him farther into the trap, hit him on the head. Hit him so hard he would never – he felt disgusted.

"Go away," he said. All his life he'd fought against violence, signed petitions, written letters, taken unpopular lines in discussions. Violence was an obscenity.

He was glad to find that even now the thought of crossing the threshold from anger to violence made him shudder. He was a civilised man.

The young man caught in the window struggled to free himself, pulling backwards, his face twisted in apprehension. It was a boy's face, narrow, soft-skinned. There was a smell of bad liquor.

"You tell your friends, go away now," George said, looking down. "Nobody's getting inside this house. That clear?"

Ridiculously, he felt sorry for the boy-man who twisted to escape. He knew how simple people could work themselves into situations they couldn't control or understand. He knew how they must have felt, when the girl went missing and then Niles turned up in the village.

If it had been Karen . . .

There was nothing he could do to this twisting head. He was a civilised man, refined to a point where physical violence was impossible, even in self-defence. If defending himself meant breaking this kid's skull then he couldn't defend himself. He was a modern man, he needed locks and doors and bolted windows and policemen. Objects defended him. He had lost the ability to stand alone and fight.

Almost wearily, he pushed the boy-man's arm.

"Leave us alone, for Christ's sake," he said, and felt a surge of relief when the boy pulled his head back.

"Here's the washing line, George," said Louise, standing in the gloom of the hall. "It's some kind of flex, you could cut it with this."

She held out the carving knife, handle first. The blade

104

gleamed in the weak light. Some men could use a thing like that.

"There isn't much point," he said. "It's hopeless. If they really want to get in we can't stop them. You might as well open the front door and ask them to step inside and help themselves to Niles."

"But you said –"

"*I* said! Don't tell me you actually listened to anything *I* said!"

"But they shot Bill Knapman!"

"It was his own fault. It's only Niles they want. If we try to fight them we'll only get hurt, you and Karen."

Louise had been almost at a point where she felt guilty, ashamed at her own bitchiness in the face of George's determination. Now he seemed to have given up.

"Do you think they'll – they'll harm Niles?"

"What else? You think they want him to play snowballs? They're crazy! We don't have a chance. If they get Niles they'll leave us alone. At least none of us will get hurt."

They both realised that there was no noise outside. They listened.

"Maybe they've gone away," she said.

"Maybe. I know, we'll phone the Inn. Why didn't I think of it before. Surely there's somebody in this goddam place who hasn't gone mad."

But when he picked up the phone it was dead. . . .

Norman Scutt, Chris Cawsey, Phillip Riddaway, Bert Voizey and Tom Hedden stood together in the rickety old shed across the lane.

"We've got to get in," Norman Scutt said, biting hard on his thumb.

He knew the others – apart from Tom Hedden – were beginning to collapse. They'd never been in prison, they couldn't imagine it would happen to them. He knew, though. Ten years for manslaughter.

"He's a funny bugger that Yank," said Cawsey, sniggering as he told them what had happened when he'd been caught halfway in the window. Norman Scutt interrupted him.

"So he knows you all right, Chris then," he said. "You're good for ten year."

"Oh aye, he knows me all right."

"And Bert and Phil and me were in the house and he knows us. And Tom. So what d'you want to do then, you lot, go home and wait for the coppers to come for us in the morning?"

"What're us standin' here for then?" Tom Hedden demanded. "I'll get in that house, I'll get that Niles and –"

"How're you getting in then, Tom? Think you're going to kick a hole in the door? Look, you buggers, us've got to use our brains. Plans. That's what counts. Us use our brains and us'll be in the clear."

"I don't think they'll send we to prison for Tom shooting Bill Knapman," said Bert Voizey.

"That's your bloody trouble, Voizey, you'm spend all your time with rats. I've been inside, haven't I? You know what it's like – in gaol? For ten year or more?" Then Norman had an inspiration. Already he saw himself as the brains behind a gang of desperate men. "Don't you lot remember what happened all them years ago in Soldier's Field? They killed that fellow then, didn't they? And nobody ever got caught. You know why? They'm knew what they were doing. They all stuck together and nobody ever breathed a whisper."

"They'm all took a turn with the knife," said Chris Cawsey.

"But if one of us gets any smart idea he can get off . . ."

"I won't say nothin'," said Bert Voizey, his voice a mixture of fear and indignation.

"All right then. Us stick together. Folk in Dando won't be tellin' the cops nothin'. They ain't goin' to take their side against us, are they?"

He knew he had them now. Phil was just a big lump with no brains. Maybe he thought he could have a go at the Yank's wife. Cawsey was just dying to get his knife into somebody. Bert Voizey was too scared to run away. Tom Hedden was like a mad bull, he was crazy to get at Niles.

And himself? He'd had as much rum as the rest but he knew he was the brains. He knew what was facing them. He knew what ten year inside meant. With his brains they'd never be caught. It would become history – like the soldier. Nobody had ever said a word to the police about the soldier. All the wives must have known. Lots of people must have known. Nobody ever told. Dando folk stuck together. They'd be heroes, for doing away with Henry Niles.

There were other thoughts going round his head. He'd been in Bristol when they hung that chap, the one that had killed the farmer. They'd hung him, the last hanging in the whole country. That night they'd battered their tin mugs on the bars and shouted and sung all night.

Sometimes they'd seen the hanging chap in the yard, exercising on his own. He'd come to chapel – they were practising carols for the Christmas service – but he'd been put behind special screens, separating him from the ordinary villains. All the time everybody had said they hated the idea of hanging a man. What was it *like* to kill somebody? Better than hitting a girl over the head? Better than getting into a posh house and turning it into a shitty mess? Better than stealing gear and going into pubs with the money and knowing you were smarter than everybody else? Better than laughing at mugs who had to work their guts out? Better than two of you getting hold of a bit of class stuff and getting her into a wood and ramming her till she would do *anything* for you?

He'd done all these things and now he remembered how he'd felt at the time.

"Right then, we'm goin' to get in that house. Phil, you have a go at the back door, Chris you go for that window you were in before. Tom's got the gun, you try the front door. I'll try and slip in the window at the other end. And Bert – you got any matches on you?"

"Yeh."

"Well then, sec if you can't get some of them curtains burning, maybe us'll smoke 'em out. That Yankee bugger won't know what hit him."

They had another pass round of the rum bottle. As they began to cross the lane Chris Cawsey's cap blew off. He slipped and fell as he tried to catch it. He laughed loudly as he scrabbled on all fours for the cap, which the wind kept blowing away from his stretching hands. . . .

Sister Brady left the casualty ward without looking at the woman in the yellow coat. She didn't want to know what Frank Pawson's wife looked like. She had just been told by the casualty ward sister that Pawson had multiple skull fractures and, almost certainly, a broken spine. Shocked as she was, she was still able to think clearly. Frank was lucky he had a wife to look after him. A thing like that could often bring people together again.

Whatever happened, she told herself she was very lucky. It

107

was the wife's duty to look after her man. Life was cruel but these things often turned out for the best. When she got a man he was going to be a proper man, not a permanent invalid.

Bobby Hedden opened the door in his stockinged feet, a black-haired boy of fifteen with a scowl on his face. With his father away and his mother sleeping and his brothers in bed and Janice missing he'd had his first chance of a proper look at his father's books. He'd accidentally discovered them hidden under some sacking on the water tank in the attic, but he'd never been alone in the house since.

He'd been up in the attic with a torch when he'd heard the noise at the door.

Standing on the doorstep was Doctor Allsopp, his coat caked with snow, blood dried hard on his forehead and cheeks. His eyes were almost closed.

"You'm had an accident, Doctor?"

"Tom's got a gun," the doctor mumbled. "Must get to the . . ." He swayed. Bobby didn't want to touch him. The doctor was important, not like them.

"I'm . . ."

The doctor began to fall, his hands clawing for a grip on the doorpost. Bobby tried to catch him but the man's weight was too much. They both fell into the kitchen, the doctor a dead weight on his legs. Bobby Hedden dragged himself free. The doctor was moaning. Bobby gripped him by the shoulders and dragged him across the kitchen floor to the battered sofa by the fire.

He had often helped his mother to pull his father on to the sofa when he'd come home drunk from the pub. First he swung the feet up, then he caught hold under the armpits and lifted his dead weight, bracing his knee under the doctor's back, wrestling him on to the sofa.

He couldn't smell drink on the doctor's breath. It must have been a crash. Where was Chris Cawsey? They couldn't have been driving very fast in that snow. Maybe the doctor had been fighting Niles the murderer? What did he mean, Tom had a gun? Of course he had, he'd gone into the backroom for it when they'd left to go to Trencher's. The doctor opened his eyes.

"Tom's got a gun –" he seemed to notice Bobby for the first time. "You run to the Inn, tell them your father's got a gun . . .

108

he's – he's gone to Trencher's, you get to the ..." Then he went out again.

Bobby didn't understand. Maybe he ought to fetch the doctor – but Dr. Allsopp *was* the doctor. What did he mean, go to the Inn? Bugger that for a lark. Somebody would be coming shortly. That reminded him he was on his own, the only chance he had of a good look at his father's books. He'd never seen pictures of women like that, hardly any clothes at all. What was his father doing with books like that on top of the water-tank? He wanted to see them again. The doctor would be all right here in front of the fire.

Bobby Hedden went back up to the attic. If anybody came he would hear them and have time to put away the books.

Snow turned to water on the doctor's hair and face and coat and trousers and rubber boots. Soon little wisps of steam hovered above the damp folds of his clothing. He didn't move.

CHAPTER TEN

Although it had been what she wanted, to let the men outside have Niles and leave them in peace, George's apparent change of mind didn't make Louise feel any less irritated. Whatever the real reason for her discontent – and she didn't really know herself – she felt as though she was swamped by a deep sense of *grudge*. It showed no signs of evaporating even now that he'd seemingly come to see things as they really were. Everything about him now irritated her. He was so damned artificial. Just for a moment she'd thought he was going to belt her and funnily enough she'd felt a sense of relief, but then he'd taken hold of himself. That was part of it, he was so damned anxious to keep control of himself. He *acted* the role of a reasonable, steady, dependable husband. In her general state of unreasonable resentment she saw this as an insult; if he was sincere he wouldn't need to act, to keep such tight control of himself.

She left him trying to get some life on the telephone and went upstairs to Karen's bedroom. She looked at her daughter with the wary eyes of a woman who had betrayal in mind and she could see herself for the bitch she was and she could find nothing loving to say.

109

"What's happening, Mother?"

"Why don't you go to sleep, Karen!"

"They keep shouting that man's name, is he a bad man? What's happened to Janice Hedden, hasn't she come back yet? I'm frightened."

"Don't be silly now. They won't be here much longer, they've probably gone away already, they were just worried about Janice, that's all."

"Did that man do something horrible to Janice? I didn't like him, he had a funny face, Mother."

"For God's sake, Karen! Go to sleep will you? I've told you there's nothing wrong, that's all I –"

The whole house seemed to be hit by one big bang. Somebody kicked the front door. At the same time there was a dull thudding noise from the other side of the house. Somewhere in the din she heard glass breaking.

"I'm scared," Karen sobbed.

Good God, she thought, what's George doing now? Why the hell isn't he speaking to them, telling them they could take Niles away?

"Stay here and don't cry," she snapped at Karen as she left the bedroom, slamming the door behind her, but forgetting to lock it.

As she crossed the upstairs landing she heard Niles moaning in the lavatory. It served him damn well right, she thought. It was the best place for him if he had to be in the house at all. She felt her temper rising.

"George! What the hell are you *doing*?"

"Christ, they're all over the place," he said, standing in the gloom of the sitting-room, a dark shape in the red glow from the fire.

"Damn you, George, I'm sick of it!"

She knew it was up to her. George was hopeless. She cursed as she caught her shin on the edge of the coffee table. She found the handle of the door into the hall.

"Where are you going, Louise?"

"I'm coming," she shouted.

George realised she was going to open the front door. He strode towards the hall, forgetting about the armchair. He lost his balance as he bumped into it and fell forward, crashing with the chair to the floor.

"Louise!"

"Stop kicking the door, damn you," she was shouting. "It's this damned chain."

George scrambled to his feet and moved towards her, his hands up to protect his face in case he ran into the open hall door.

He got to her just as she was slipping the chain catch along its slide. He caught hold of her wrists and pulled her away from the door.

"Let me go!"

"What are you doing? Those guys are crazy!"

Her voice was grimly controlled.

"George, if you don't open that door right now I'm going to leave you. I'm not joking. Open that door and let them take that man out of this house or I'm going."

"But they'll —"

"Did you hear me? It's *him* they want, that thing upstairs. Make up your mind, George, he goes or I go."

He knew she was right. He was a civilised man and there was nothing he could do but open the door and let them drag Niles out of the house. Tomorrow they'd pay, he'd make sure of that. But tonight, now, they were like a pack of wolves and there was nothing he could do.

"All right," he said. "I'll tell him."

He shot the bolt and turned the Yale handle. The door opened about four inches until the chain went tight.

"Tell them to stop it," he said, putting his face to the gap. "You can have Niles. But if you harm him I'm going to make sure the police know exactly who you are, you and your pals."

Tom Hedden had his hand against the door, shoving at it.

"Did you hear what I said?" George asked. He knew they would harm Niles, he knew exactly what they'd do to him, but nobody would blame him.

"Let me in the door." Tom Hedden's voice was a snarl of hate.

"I said you aren't going to do anything to him."

Tom Hedden was maddened by rage and drink and frustration. He rammed his shoulder against the door. George let go of his hold. The door pulled hard on the chain and then rebounded, the Yale lock clicking as it slammed shut. Tom Hedden hit it again with his shoulder.

"I' show you, dirty Yank bastard," he roared,

111

Before he could reach the lock handle he was deafened by a noise that hit him and Louise like a blow on the face. For a second they stood still, the deafening boom pounding in their heads. Then, acting instinctively, he grabbed at Louise and pushed her towards the sitting-room. Like a dream in which nameless horrors are instantly recognisable, he knew that the man outside had fired his shotgun. Louise said something but his ears were full of a dull roar. He tried to speak but he couldn't hear his own words.

They clung together in the shelter of the wall. . . .

When they heard the boom of the shotgun the others came running round to the front of the house.

"Open the bloody door!" Hedden kept shouting. When Norman Scutt realised what had happened he knew the answer to one thing that had bothered him. Tom Hedden's shotgun would do any killing they had to do. Hedden was out of his mind, mad enough to shoot the lot of them. The thought made him happier. You had to think of Number One. He knew what they had to do if they weren't going to be locked up for ten years, but he hadn't reckoned on killing them himself. Better for Tom – and Cawsey – to do it. That way, even if they were caught, he could get out of it. He'd say Hedden had the gun and *he'd* been trying to stop him.

"You got more cartridges?" he asked.

"Aye, some," said Tom Hedden.

"You'd better get a couple in then. You could blow that door down, eh?"

He and Voizey and Phil Riddaway stood back to watch what Tom Hedden would do next. Chris Cawsey slipped along the front of the house. Tom Hedden wasn't going to get all the fun.

It was as if the blast of the gun had changed everything. Louise stood limp, her chest shaking with sobs. George kept swallowing until his ears cleared. That shell would have blasted the head off his body!

"Where's that cord you had?" he said. They'd killed Bill Knapman and they didn't care if they killed anybody else. Those were the wolves he'd been going to throw Niles to! For a moment he felt ashamed. Then angry. He'd been weak. He'd let Louise talk him into opening the door, ready to hand over

Niles. They would have shot Niles as soon as he was through the door.

"Where is it?" he demanded.

She went on sobbing. It was his fault, for letting her dominate him. That thought made him even angrier. He shook her.

"The cord! And the knife!"

She sniffed.

"I think – I – it was beside the telephone, I'm scared, George, what'll they do to us?"

"Stand there. Don't move an inch!"

He ducked and ran past the front door, raising his arm to feel about on the small window ledge. He touched the knife blade and then the thin washing line. Still crouching he ducked back.

"Get into the sitting-room," he hissed. In the soft red light from the fire he took the hank of plastic flex and began cutting it into two-foot lengths, jerking the knife edge through the thin line.

"I'm going to tie up the windows," he said, controlling a note of hysteria which threatened to turn his words into a babble. "You wait right here. Understand?"

"Don't leave me alone, George," she moaned.

This time, when the shotgun went off, he had been subconsciously expecting it. Mingled with the boom was the sound of wood splintering. Louise jumped with shock, letting out a thin scream.

"Get a grip on yourself," he said. "They can't shoot their way through the door, it's solid. You know what'll happen if they get in now, they'll shoot us all. They've gone too far to back down now. Do you understand that?"

She began to sob again. Acting calmly, his left hand feeling for a grip in the hair at the back of her neck, he put the flex and the knife on the coffee table. Then he hit her across the face, two meaty slaps which made his palm tingle. She was about to scream, but he tightened his grip on her hair and pulled her face close to his.

"Shut up, Louise!" he said. "I don't care about *you*. They'll kill Karen, too, that's all I care about. Do you want that, Louise?"

She breathed with sharp, shallow gulps.

"Do what I tell you or I'll smack you silly," he said. "Stay here. I'm going to the study."

113

Again he ran doubled up past the front door, moving on his toes so that the man with the gun wouldn't hear him and try another blast. As he ran he remembered Knapman jumping about in the snow. Reaching the study door, he thumbed the catch as quietly as he could. Once he had this window tied up he would do the kitchen.

The door opened. He stayed in his crouch, looking at the billowing curtain. He heard voices. The knife and flex in his right hand, he moved along like an ape, the knuckle of his left hand acting as a third foot, his shoulder brushing the wall. He stopped just before he reached the window. The voices were only a foot or two away.

"You get in this time?"

"Aye, I know the catch now."

"They'll be hiding from the gun. Get in and slip along and open the door."

"Tell that bloody Hedden not to fire at me. It's them us want to get."

"I'll be there. And Chris –"

"Yeah?"

"Don't do nothin' to them till we're all in. Like Soldier's Field, right? We're all in it together and we're all right. Bert's kind of panicky, give him half a chance and he's off out of it. We don't want that. He does his turn like the rest of us, he won't say nothin'. all right?"

"Yeh."

Soldier's Field? George heard the other man moving along on the other side of the wall. Soldier's Field? Gregory Allsopp had told them about that. Some guy, years ago, they'd found him murdered in a field, supposed to have raped a village girl or something. Real local colour, Gregory had called it, what was that he'd said, making a joke out of it, something silly about primeval passions and dark blood, some nonsense? What did it mean? Above his head he heard the movements of the man, scrabbling of a body against the wall, then something inside the room, heavy breathing.

He waited until the panting breath seemed to be just above his head, then he stood up.

"Don't move," he said, "don't say anything."

In the light from the upstairs window he could see it was the same guy he'd already caught half through the window. He caught hold of the wrist that was feeling for the catch. He

114

pulled until the arm was fully extended across the window ledge.

"See that?" he said, holding the carving knife close to the man's face. "Make one move and I'll shove it down your throat."

He didn't know where the idea came from. It was just something he found himself doing, as though from habit. He made a loop of flex round the wrist, the knife still in the palm of his right hand, the blade waving about at the guy's face. Tying a knot he jerked the arm up against the centre post and slipped the flex round the swan's neck catch.

They were battering at the front door again. That was all right, even if they burst the lock and the bolt the chain would hold them. They'd need a bazooka to shoot a hole in that heavy wood.

He tied the wrist tight to the catch, the guy grunting with pain as his arm was twisted above his head.

"Shove your other hand in the window – and don't make any noise!"

"You'm cut him on the glass," Chris Cawsey moaned as George grabbed the other hand and dragged it through the jagged hole.

"Too bad – I told you to keep quiet, didn't I?"

Then he had both hands trussed together, the thin plastic line cutting into the guy's wrists.

"That hurting you?" he asked.

"My neck's on glass."

"Good. I hope you slit your throat."

"It won't be *my* throat's cut," Cawsey said. George remembered he was carrying a knife. He wondered if he would have been able to use it.

Now for the kitchen. He could hear them outside as he ducked by the front door. How many blasts of buckshot would it take?

Now that his mind was concentrating on the need to keep them out of the house he found he was able to think of it as a place to defend. The kitchen, with its big window, was an obvious weak spot.

"You'd better get upstairs and watch Karen," he said to Louise. "Make sure all the lights are switched on, I've got to be able to see them – they won't see me. I'm going to tie the kitchen window up, they can still climb in but it won't be so

115

easy. Is the outside kitchen door locked?"

"The door to the porch is locked, I bolted it," she said. Her voice seemed to have lost all trace of hysteria.

"Stand on the stairs there till I come back. If they try these windows shout!"

As his fingers looped the flex round the two catches, tying as many knots as the length of line would allow, he listened for footsteps. None came. They still thought the front door was their best bet. What did that mean – about Soldier's Field? *Like Soldier's Field . . .?*

There. It would take them time to untie those knots. To get in they'd have to smash the glass and squeeze through. That wouldn't be too difficult, but at least he'd have warning. The guy he'd tied up would block the study window, they couldn't get past him to untie his hands.

He listened. Still no sounds outside. He decided it was a chance worth taking. He opened the inside kitchen door, holding the bolt with both hands so that it wouldn't rattle. Ready to jump back inside at the slightest sound, he eased the porch door to. It had a big, old bolt and a mortice lock. He slid the bolt home and then turned the mortice key.

Then he had the inside door bolted and locked. That was one way they'd never get into the house. Time – if he could hold them up long enough *somebody* would come. Where the hell were the police? Surely *they* had ways of beating the snow? Where was Gregory Allsopp for Chrissake?

He remembered something else. From Branksheer's account of a farm-workers' riot in Lincolnshire. Branksheer had been staying overnight in the local inn when the rioters had tried to set fire to it, because they thought he was the landlord's new agent. It had seemed a jolly, bucolic comedy – to read about, Branksheer in his nightgown, people yelling out of upstairs windows . . . and the serving people, throwing pots of boiling water over the arsonists!

He didn't have a gun. He remembered a phrase from the army, make your defences credible. Establish positions – then talk. Not that he could ever throw boiling water over a man. But it would be credible enough, something these maniac yokels would understand.

Under the sink there was a sliding wooden door and behind that four or five pots and pans of various sizes. He pulled out three and filled them with hot water from the sink tap. He put

116

them on the *Aga* hot-plates. A balance of terror, that was it. They had a gun, he had boiling water. A balance of force. They'd go away when they realised the house wasn't defence-less. They didn't know he could not cross that dividing line.

When he got back into the sitting-room, Louise was still at the foot of the stairs, crouching down on the second step.

He quickly tied up the dining-room window. It was prob-ably just large enough for a man to crawl through, but it wouldn't be a quick job.

"Did I put that poker thing down in here?" he asked Louise as he went to the sitting-room window. Like the others at the front of the house it was set in the thick cob wall, four panes of glass on two frames opening outwards from a centre post. Once he had the two frames tied securely to the centre post they could enter only through one of the broken panes – about eighteen inches square. Unless, of course, they got hold of an axe and smashed the wooden framework. Then they'd be able to more or less walk in, the windows being only three feet at the most from the ground.

"Didn't you have it when you were phoning?"

"Yeah."

It wasn't much, just a thin steel affair with a kind of fork at the end for lifting off the ash door of the *Esse*. But it was some-thing to hold in his hand. Reassuring. Man's age-old impulse to hold a stick.

"Right then," he said. "Let's see what they –"

Glass smashed in the kitchen.

"Wait here," he said. "Watch those windows."

He moved quietly into the kitchen doorway. He felt confi-dent now. In the light thrown from the upstairs lavatory win-dow he could see a man standing sideways on to the window, his arm and shoulder pushing through the broken pane to get at the catches.

He moved along the wall. There was just a chance the guy with the gun was out there. He reached the corner, his chest pressed against the wall. He lifted the thin poker and smacked it down, hard, on the man's hand. It was like admonishing an unruly child, a blow that would warn, not hurt.

The man cursed.

"You won't get in that way," George called out. The arm was pulled back. George dropped to a crouch and listened. Nothing.

He felt much better. It was a bizarre situation – one that would seem unbelievable tomorrow morning, when daylight came – yet he'd handled it as well as anybody could have hoped. Soon they'd go away....

When she heard the terrible boom of the shotgun Karen Magruder had shoved her head deep down under the blankets and put her hands over her ears and pressed her face into the sheet and screamed and screamed and screamed. Neither Mother nor Daddy came to see her. Eventually she screamed herself to a state of exhaustion.

Then she had found she needed the toilet. She called for her mother, but she didn't come. When she'd been about five she'd gone through a spell of bed-wetting and she still remembered how nasty that had been, Mother and Daddy talking about it, taking her to see doctors and other men who'd asked her lots and lots of *awful* questions.

Frightened as she was with all the noise and shouting downstairs, she was even more frightened of wetting the bed. At last, when she could hold herself no longer, even with her legs crossed and her knees shaking violently, she slipped out of bed. Downstairs she heard her father's voice. It sounded normal. Perhaps it was some kind of horrid *English* game – she couldn't understand why grown-ups would make so much noise.

Pushing her feet into her slippers she went to the door. The last time Mother had been upstairs she hadn't locked the door. And she hadn't said she wasn't to go to the toilet. If she went *very* quickly, on tip-toe, they wouldn't know.

When her slippers went clop-clop on the wooden floor of the upstairs corridor she took them off and went on in her bare feet. The light was on. Downstairs she heard Daddy say something, and Mother say something back.

She reached the landing and waited for a moment. She tip-toed across the landing. Nobody came up the stairs. She climbed the two steps up to the bathroom level one by one, waiting each time to hear if there was anybody coming.

Then she tip-toed past the bathroom door and put her fingers on the handle of the lavatory door. She turned it slowly. The door wouldn't open. Looking down she saw that it was bolted. Why had Mummy done that?

She slipped the bolt very carefully, shivering with cold, her knees pressed together, trying to control herself.

"You've not to keep me in here," said a man's voice.

It was the horrible man they'd brought home! He had no trousers on. He pulled the door away from her. His face was *awful*. His eyes were staring right into her.

This time, when she screamed, there was no mattress to deaden the sound.

CHAPTER ELEVEN

Karen's scream went through George's body like ten thousand volts. It hit his brain like a searing blast of white-hot light. He had seen Knapman shot, windows broken, men attacking his house, men climbing in his windows – but he had seen all these things with the eyes of the man he thought he was. The civilised man who stood on this side of the threshold, seen them as though they were a part of a ridiculous dream. Everything he had done until now had been done consciously, almost in spite of his instinctive disbelief that such things *could* happen.

The scream filled his head. It called directly to muscle and flesh. As he jumped the stairs, two at a time, everything else was forgotten. His daughter had screamed. There was no thinking. Behind him he heard Louise shouting something, but she didn't matter. Not then. It was *his* body that was in pain.

At the top of the stairs he saw Karen and Niles, close together in the open lavatory door. Karen was still throwing out that blinding, *physical* noise, her little girl's body jack-knifing uncontrollably from the waist as though in a demented tantrum.

His eye took in the scene and his body acted. He jumped the two landing steps and hurled himself at Niles.

Coming up the stairs behind him, Louise tripped and rapped her shin on a stair. She didn't notice any pain. She heard George shouting, his feet pounding on the wooden floor. He wasn't shouting recognisable words. It was a terrifying, full-pitched, demoniac roar.

Karen didn't seem to have seen her father. She stood with her body bent forward from the waist, still yelling, her eyes closed, her hands clenched into little fists which she held near her ears.

George towered in the doorway above Niles, whose face

was wide-eyed, surprised, frozen in shock. She saw him hit Niles with the poker, his right elbow rising and blocking off the light, a great shadow sliding up the wall. Louise caught Karen round the waist and lifted her up, turning her into the hollow of her neck.

"It's all right, darling," she kept saying, pressing the little girl's contorted face into her own body. She hurried down the corridor to Karen's bedroom.

George hit Niles twice across the forehead with the thin poker. Niles held his arms above his head, letting out startled yelps. George felt the inadequacy of the poker – there was no weight in it, not enough weight to smash into the man's skull.

Then he stopped – arm slowing in mid air. Why was he hitting this little, trembling man?

"Did you touch her?"

"It wasn't my fault," Niles blubbered, his body going slack, slipping to the floor. "It wasn't my fault."

George didn't bother to think of all the things that could have happened or why. Niles had to be tied down in some way, locked away, put out of action. He thought of tying him up, but there was no more left of the washing line. The attic!

"Pick up that blanket," he ordered Niles. At the same time he reached up to the ceiling, where a folding ladder was fastened by a short lever. Shifting the poker to his left hand he pulled the lever and caught the end rung of the ladder. his knees, blubbering, helpless. George eased between the ladder and the wall and picked Niles up, right arm round his waist, no more trouble than a baby. Than Karen!

He got round the other side of the ladder again, pushing Niles through the narrow space, not caring whether he got hurt or not. He bent his knees and jerked Niles up on to his right shoulder. He dropped the poker on the floor and climbed the ladder, head twisting to the side so that he could see the bolt which fastened down the attic trapdoor.

He pulled out the bolt and went up another rung, using his head to push up the wooden flap. Up there it was dark and warm and musty. He climbed another step, his shoulders level with the attic floor. He jerked Niles up and half-shoved him, half-unloaded him on to the bare planks of wood.

"Don't make a move till I come for you," he said. Niles sat on the floor, legs crossed awkwardly beneath him. George threw up the dangling end of the blanket.

George left him there, closing out the light as he went backwards down the narrow ladder, his head holding the weight of the trapdoor. Then he rammed home the bolt and dropped back on to the landing floor. Bending down he took hold of the bottom rung of the ladder and lifted it up towards the ceiling. He held its weight with his left hand while he closed the lever that held it in place.

That took care of Niles!

There was a nagging thought in his mind. He ran along the corridor.

"You didn't lock this door, did you?" he shouted to Louise.

She looked up from Karen's bed. Karen was crying. Louise looked frightened.

"I'm sorry, I must have forgotten –"

"You stupid –"

He thought of locking them both in the room. No, he needed Louise downstairs. If they tried to come in different windows at once he needed her to stay in the sitting-room and shout to him.

Needed? He didn't need her, she was his wife, it was her place to help him. She needed him!

It was the first time in his married life that he could say this and know it to be true.

"Come on," he said. "Karen. You better stop crying now. If you want to help please keep quiet. There's nothing to be scared of, nobody's going to hurt you."

Louise hesitated about leaving Karen but he jerked his head impatiently. When he had locked the door he looked for a place to hide the key.

"Those guys were saying something about Soldier's Field," he said softly, bending down. They hadn't carpeted the upstairs corridor because Louise had said the wood was particularly attractive. Between the thick shiny planks were uneven spaces, the general effect being of ancient – but not very skilful – craftmanship. He tested the spaces with the end of the key until he found one that satisfied him. He tapped it out of sight and then levered it out again with his finger-nail. The lock to Karen's room was one of the strongest in the house. Without the key they'd have a helluva job to get in.

"What about Soldier's Field?" she asked.

"I dunno. You tell me what it means. They said, 'like Soldier's Field'. Mean anything to you? I remember Gregory Allsopp saying something –"

"That was the kitchen!"

He'd heard it, too.

"Come on."

He ran the length of the corridor. This time he wouldn't play about.

"Wait here," he called to Louise. "Shout if they try the other windows."

Louise stood at the foot of the stairs, looking across the dimly-lit sitting-room. In the ring of light thrown round the outside of the house from the upstairs windows she could see falling snowflakes. She knew they were in some kind of danger but that wasn't the uppermost thought in her mind. George had hit her! He wasn't acting like George at all. For once he was telling *her* what to do. It was as though she had been relieved of a burden that she'd been carrying for a long time. *George* was in control. . . .

Norman Scutt had told Phil Riddaway to bash a way through the kitchen window and Phil had found a length of heavy wood in the coal shed. First he smashed in the glass. Then he'd felt round the centre-post of the window for the catches, but they were tied up with some kind of flex. His big, blunt fingers could make no impression on the knot. He swung the wood at the horizontal part of the framework, once, twice . . . it cracked at the third blow. He took hold of it and cracked the wood with his hands. That opened one half of the window.

When George came into the kitchen, Phil had one foot over the sill, his head inside the window, his shoulders heaving through the narrow space.

"GET OUT OF MY HOUSE," George roared. He struck at the man's head with the thin poker, flailing blows which stung the palm of his hand as the thin steel rapped on Riddaway's skull.

"Get off," Phil snarled, trying to grab hold of the poker. With only one hand inside the window he was at a disadvantage. Each time he loosened his grip on the centre-post to snatch at the poker he felt he was losing balance. The poker hit him on the face. It bit into his skin. He cursed and tried to swipe at George. The light was against him and his arm swung at shadows.

Knowing he couldn't really hurt the guy, not seriously,

George slashed again and again at his head. Then Phil lost his hold and fell backwards, his right boot shooting into the air as he slipped backwards on to the ground. George grasped hold of the foot which stuck up above the window ledge, forcing it against the sill, making it impossible for Phil Riddaway to get to his feet.

"Next time you get boiling water in your face," he grunted, giving the ankle a twist. Then he shoved it out of the window, sending Riddaway on to his back in the snow.

He waited, moving back a few steps out of the light. The big man scrambled to his feet and went away. George walked quickly back through the dining-room.

"I think I heard them – in the study," Louise whispered.

"I tied one up. They're trying to get him loose. Lucky they aren't too clever. With that gun they could –"

"George! What did you say about Soldier's Field?"

"I told you, I heard them saying, that young one with the fancy hair, they said, 'like Soldier's Field'. I didn't –"

"George, that was where they murdered a soldier, before the first war."

"I know. But –"

"Gregory told me. It's in books and things. They killed him because he raped a village girl. They never got caught."

"Well, it couldn't be these guys, they're all too young."

"Don't you understand! There was a whole lot of them. The police could never get anybody to tell them –"

"I know all that."

"You don't understand. Gregory said it was because they were all in it that they never got caught."

"You mean –"

"They shot Bill Knapman, George! They've done one murder, they'll go to gaol anyway!"

He knew then what Soldier's Field meant. He wasn't up against a few crazy drunks. They weren't only after Niles! They wanted to kill him – and Karen and Louise, too. They couldn't hang anyway. Without witnesses –

"I need something," he said. This damn poker was like a toy pistol against an elephant. God, he knew now the attraction of guns. What did they have in the house? A chair? No, too heavy, there wasn't enough room to swing one. A broom? No.

123

"Keep out of line of the window," he said. "Isn't there anything heavy?"

It was then that Bert Voizey, pressing himself against the wall under the dining-room window, struck a match and cupped it between both hands as he rose, slowly. The wind had blown out three matches but this time he kept it alight until his hands were through the broken pane. Like smoking out rats. He could do this, let Norman and Hedden finish it. He would have run away long ago, but he was a crafty man and he knew what they'd do if they got caught.

Bert Voizey's father had been one of the men who'd hacked the soldier's head off in the field. Bert had always guessed this, but it wasn't till the old man was dying that he'd started to talk about it. *Us all done him, 'e deserved her, us niver told nobody . . . any man talkt an' us'll do him, sure enuff. . . .*

He got the thin gauze curtain going then held it against the folds of the heavy curtain.

"Hey, Norman," he hissed. "Her's burnin' now."

Norman came along the front of the house, leaving Chris Cawsey still tied to the window of the study.

"Come on, Tom," he shouted. It would have been easier if he'd had the shotgun, for Tom Hedden was too crazed to follow anybody else's plan. However, he did leave the front door, which he'd been trying to force with a big shepherd's pocket-knife, the three cartridges having made little impression. Norman was just as glad it was Tom who had the gun. If things went wrong he could put it on to Tom.

"He'll come to put her out," he said to Tom. "You keep the gun on him. We'll tell him to open the door, less the house burns down."

"Mibbe he's got a gun of his own like?" said Bert. "Them yanks all got guns they say."

"Nah, he ain't got no gun, he's just a bigmouth."

Louise saw the new light flickering on the wall of the dining-room. She nudged George.

"They've started a fire," he hissed. "The dirty bastards. There's water on the *Aga,* you get it. And keep down, there's enough light for them to see us."

Louise darted across the dining-room.

If only he had something heavy. Some kind of weapon. Christ, to think of all the arguments he'd had back in the States with people who kept guns in the house to keep out housebreakers. A phrase went through his head: There's no burglary in Texas.

He'd stopped thinking about thresholds and divides. Since Karen's scream he'd forgotten all that. If he'd had a gun in his hand now he would have shot their heads off.

Louise slipped along the wall, holding a heavy pan of steaming water. He moved up the dining-room wall, ready to throw the water over the flames. The curtain wasn't burning very quickly – not yet. It would be wet with snow blown through the broken panes of glass.

"You'm don't move," came the hard voice from outside. "I'll shoot you there. You'm go round and open the door."

The light was against him now, the glare of the flames preventing him seeing out of the window. They could see him, a barn-door target for a shotgun at that range.

"Okay," he called. He turned and made the door to the sitting-room. He stopped, pressing his back to the wall. He thought he heard them moving. The curtain light was brighter now, flickering shadows racing up and down the white walls of the dining-room.

"Keep behind the stair wall, Louise, they're ready to shoot," he whispered.

Then he ran back into the dining-room and dropped behind the long, scrubbed-wood dining-table. He remembered moving it when they first came to the house. He put down the pot of water and got his shoulder under the end of the table. He stood up, hands guiding it up and on to its other end. He shoved it towards the window, knocking over a chair. They *must* hear that and come back. The table threatened to overturn. Somebody shouted, but he caught it and kicked it forward, wood scraping on stone. Then it was in front of the window, end up, a tall, narrow shield. He jumped into the corner. The curtains were now on fire all up one side.

"Open the door or I'll blow you to ..."

He didn't hear any more. Using the table as cover, he ran in a crouch and picked up the pot of water. It felt pretty hot still.

The noise of the gun was like a kick on the ear. For a moment he felt numbed. The table began to collapse towards him. He dodged to one side and then made the corner of the wall again. Changing the pot into his right hand, he got it into position.

"YAHHH!" It was a noise to make, a bawl of defiance. The water went out through the window. At the same time he dropped the pot and grabbed at the curtains, holding his stomach against the wall. His palms closed on burning material, but he felt no pain. He tore the curtain down from its brass rail, dragging it on to the floor. Somebody yelped outside. A yelp of pain. He hoped the bastard had got the boiling water right on the kisser.

Then the flames were out. He wrestled with the curtain rod, until he could wrench it away from the wall. Now there was nothing they could set fire to. He'd have to tear the curtains down from the other windows.

He slipped along the wall, ducking when he came to the sideboard. Then he was back in the shelter of the sitting-room door.

"I think I got one," he said to Louise. "Pity we don't having boiling oil."

The water had caught Bert Voizey on the chin and neck, some of it running down on to his chest. It hadn't been boiling by the time it was thrown, but his skin felt as though it was being torn off his body by barbed wire. He went on yelping and screaming and tearing at his clothes for several minutes, until the pain subsided into mere agony.

For a few moments he stood still, his chest heaving, a dull moan coming out of his mouth with each desperate breath.

"Give I the gun, give I the gun," he suddenly yelled, trying to pull it out of Tom Hedden's hands. "I'll kill the bastard, I'll kill him."

If they had been at all doubtful up till then about what Norman Scutt said they had to do, the men outside Trencher's Farm were now ready to tear the house to pieces with their bare hands. Each one of them knew that water could have blinded Bert Voizey. Or blinded them.

After they'd had a cup of tea, Sergeant Wills asked Picken if he thought he was fit to travel.

"It's my feet," said Picken, grimacing with pain. He'd taken off his boots and socks and put them in a big enamel basin filled with tepid water.

Davies seemed all right, teeth still rattling with the cold, but so were his own.

"If us had a phone you'm could phone the station like," said the farmer. "But us don't, like."

"Yes, I know," said Sergeant Wills.

"There's a phone at the Endacotts," said the farmer. "You'm could phone from there like."

The farm with the phone was about a mile farther on. Sergeant Wills thought for a moment, looking at Picken's feet. These young coppers were easy knocked out. When *he'd* started there was only him to cover three parishes, him and his bike. A little bit of snow didn't put him off in those days. But that was before they had cars and radios and scooters and all this modern paraphernalia.

"We don't want to go in that weather, Sarnt," said Davies. "It's not doing any good, us going down with exposure."

Sergeant Wills knew that the inspector wouldn't blame them for not going on. Nobody expected policemen to be heroes these days. Ordinary men, that's what they were supposed to be. Only he remembered the old days when there was him and his bike and gangs of poachers who'd as soon gaff a copper as a salmon. There had been no radios or cars when he'd got that call to the Fearncombe farm, when the Fearncombes' daft son Nelson had gone wild with his father's .22 and shot at the postman and the doctor because he thought they were coming to take him for the army.

"You stay here, Picken," he said, standing up, reaching for his helmet. "Davies and me'll push on a bit. Look bad if we're sitting here drinking tea and Niles is at Dando. Thanks for the tea, Missus."

Davies knew better than argue with Sergeant Wills. Picken groaned and bent down to look at his feet, anxious to make it clear *they* were stopping him, not anything else.

"Should take us no more'n another hour," the sergeant said, cheerfully, as he and Constable Davies looked out across the snow-drenched yard. "Come on, lad, a policeman's lot is not a happy one."

Davies groaned. He'd joined the police to get into plain-clothes work, not to play bloody Eskimos.

It was just after eight when they left the farmyard. Sergeant Wills thought they'd be doing well to reach Dando by half past nine. Provided they didn't lose their way again....

When Gregory Allsopp opened his eyes it was to find his

127

feet on fire and a child yelling in another room. He could smell rubber. Pulling himself to a sitting position he found he was stretched on a sofa in front of a range fire. Smoke was rising from the soles of his rubber boots. Cursing with pain he dragged his feet off the sofa and pulled off his boots. The soles had gone soft.

"Is anybody there?" he shouted.

Then he realised his head was thundering with pain. For a moment he thought he was going to faint. He lay back with his eyes closed until he felt better.

"HALLO?" he called.

The child went on bawling. Where the hell was he?

It all came back when Bobby Hedden, a strange look of guilt on his flushed face, came into the farmhouse kitchen.

"Good God," the doctor exclaimed. "How long have I been here like this?"

"Bout half an hour," said Bobby. The doctor knew that look on a boy's face. He made a mental shrug. The important thing was . . . what was the important thing?

"Good God! Your father hit me with a gun!"

Bobby Hedden stared uncomprehendingly. Gregory Allsopp knew bloody well the boy wasn't as thick as he looked. What was he to do?

"Is it still snowing?" he asked, closing his eyes and shaking his head.

"Oh aye."

He made a superhuman effort and stood up. It was as though his brains were trying to hammer their way out of his skull.

"Why did your father take a gun?" he asked, lifting up his boots. They had stopped smoking. "You could've taken them off, I was almost on fire."

"Oh."

"Why did your father take a gun?"

"For that lunatic, weren't it?"

"Oh Christ!"

The child went on bawling.

"Go and see to him," he told Bobby. "I'm going to the Magruders' house."

"Be hard walkin', won't her?" said Bobby.

"The cold air may help my head. If anybody comes tell them where I've gone. Now go and see what's wrong in there."

His dizziness soon disappeared in the wind and snow. Tom

Hedden had gone out of his mind. Janice! Cawsey had come to say this Niles chap was at Trencher's Farm. Tom had fetched the gun. He must have gone mad. What the hell did he think he was going to do with the gun? What time was it? He couldn't see his watch. There was a short-cut, across Soldier's Field and one of Colonel Scott's fields to the village.

Trying not to fall into the ditch he kept to the left side of the road, in the comparative shelter of the high bank. When he came to the gate which led to the path across the fields he floundered in waist-high snow blown through the gap.

He scrambled up the verge to the five-barred gate. It was only five or ten minutes since he'd left the farm but already the terrible chill had penetrated his clothes. His fingers pulsed with a numbing ache. Blood pounded where Tom Hedden had hit him with the gun. He had to squint to protect his eyes against the snow and wind and the strain gave him a new pain, a nagging throb behind his forehead. As he climbed the gate he looked for lights in the village, something he could use as a guide across the fields. There were pinpoints of light in the darkness but he could not be sure whether they were windows or spots in front of his eyes.

It was ridiculous to think that he could get lost, crossing two fields which he knew as well as he knew his back garden. He climbed down from the gate and started across the slow rise of the hill, the gale occasionally catching him full on the chest and threatening to blow him head over heels.

He saw dark shapes which he took for certain houses or trees. Yet when he blinked and peered again, to make sure, there were other shapes in different places. Or no shapes at all. Just blackness. He had heard of men dying on the Moor in blizzards like this – when they were less than fifty feet from houses. But that couldn't happen to a sensible man. He could still feel that his left foot was on higher ground than his right. That meant he was crossing the face of the sloping field in the right direction.

It was then he tripped. His boots came down on something, a lump? A dead sheep? He fell sideways, his right ankle turning awkwardly.

As he struggled to right himself his hand touched something hard. His fingers probed in snow. Numb as they were, he found he was exploring the shape of a shoe. Trying to get up off his knees his right ankle gave way and he fell again. Wanting to

129

cry out with the numbing pain in his hands, he got on all fours and felt about in the snow.

Using his hands almost like blunt instruments he pulled and pushed at the deadweight until he was in no doubt that he had found Janice Hedden.

CHAPTER TWELVE

When George went into the study to tear down the curtains he saw the shapes of two men crowded into the window opening.

Phil Riddaway had smashed another pane to get at the line which held Chris Cawsey's hands tight to the window catches. He was twisting his great arms in the small space so that he could work the blade of his pocket-knife between Cawsey's wrists and the flex.

Knowing now they were willing to shoot at him through the windows, George moved quietly along the wall until he was ready to strike.

"That's one of the boogers," Phil Riddaway said, grunting with the strain of his unnatural position.

George stepped out from behind the wall and jabbed at the big man's face with the thin poker.

"GAAAH," roared Riddaway, throwing up an elbow to protect himself.

Knowing he couldn't do real harm with the poker, George struck with full force, whipping the thin length of steel across Riddaway's head and hands, hoping to knock the knife to the floor.

"LOUISE! GET THE WATER!" he yelled.

Immediately Riddaway tried to pull himself out of the small square of wood, slivers of glass cracking as his elbows and shoulders twisted and turned.

"Get me out of it, Phil." Cawsey fought with his free hand to tear away the cord that held his other wrist to the centre post. Phil Riddaway couldn't see into the room. He didn't want boiling water on his face. With a wrench he dragged himself free and lurched back from the window. Cawsey went on yelping for help.

"Keep out of this window or your friend gets his face boiled!" George shouted.

By now he had a clear picture of the house's weak spots. Like a good siege commander, he thought. The study window was one, if they could get the guy untied. The kitchen window was the other. The study and the kitchen, the two extremities. If they cottoned on and launched attacks on both at the same time he wouldn't be able to run back and forth. One of them would get in. Then what?

Did they really intend to murder them all? Maybe they should retreat up the stairs – into the attic with Niles! Once the trapdoor went down they could never get up the folding steps. One man up there could sit on top of an army.

But they'd set fire to the curtains. A big blaze would suit them – and in the attic there was no escape hole.

"You hear that?" he snarled at Cawsey. "Tell your friends you get burned if they try to touch you."

Cawsey pulled and tugged his wrist until the line cut into his skin. Like an animal in a trap, George thought. Only we're in the trap.

He moved through the hall, ducking quickly past the small window at the telephone. A man couldn't get through there, but a shotgun shell could.

Still, he felt confident enough. And still he hadn't needed to cross any stupid thresholds. Tomorrow morning he'd be the man who had done the right thing. He'd have saved Niles, he wouldn't even have used excessive violence on the mob. He remembered now what this situation reminded him of, the tree-house he'd made when he was a boy, in the deformed oak at the bottom of Wainwright's meadow. Once he'd pulled up the rope ladder he'd been perfectly alone, the world shut out, safe in a shell.

"I suppose Karen's all right now?" he said to Louise, who still crouched at the foot of their stairs.

"Will I go up and see?"

Louise's voice made him feel even more confident. It was a quiet, *asking* voice, the smart-alec tone completely gone. He felt that he loved her a great deal. Maybe this had been a lucky –

SMASH!

Glass smashing, wood cracking, heavy bump. The kitchen!

Three of them, Scutt, Voizey and Riddaway, had found a

131

long plank of heavy wood in the shed across the road. It was Norman Scutt who'd known what to do with it, smash in the frame-work of the kitchen window. A battering-ram.

George held himself against the wall as he looked round into the kitchen. He could see the plank, jutting into the room, the three men pulling at the other end for another go. They'd missed the centre-post. Where was the guy with the shotgun?

That's what Norman Scutt wanted to know.

"Tom! Here, Tom!"

George knew he had only seconds to act. There was no sign of the gun. He strode to the *Aga*. The two remaining pans *had* to be boiling now. He got his fingers round a handle, his skin feeling the heat of the water. Holding it out from his hip he ran to the window and heaved it at them.

As he dived against the wall he heard two men yelling. In the split second after he'd swung the pan at the gaping window he thought he'd seen the smooth spew of water reaching them. Too low for their faces, though. Hands maybe. He had to get out of the kitchen before the other one, the shotgun, had a chance to spray the room with shot.

"Where is he?" That was him, the one who'd shot Bill Knapman.

"My hands, it's my hands!" somebody else was roaring.

"Shoot him, shoot him," Norman Scutt shouted.

George lay against the wall under the window. If he made a jump for the door they'd see him.

"Shoot him!"

"I can't see nothin'. Where's he gone?"

"Give me the bloody gun!"

"I'll get him, I'll get him, where's he gone?"

Norman Scutt tried to pull the shotgun away from Tom Hedden. George heard them grunting. Slowly raising his head he peered over the window sill. Perhaps they were falling out among themselves? Divide and conquer? He waited till the gun was pointing at the ground.

"There he is!"

He reached the kitchen doorway as Tom Hedden swung the shotgun up into the window. He threw himself face first in a dive for the shelter of the wall. His shoulder hit the solid wall. He crashed to the floor then kicked himself forward.

If the other shots had been deafening, this time it seemed as if the explosion had been fired off inside his own head. It

132

wasn't just a noise, it was a pulverising force. When his face touched the floor he could have crashed down from a great height such was the hammering sensation.

He couldn't tell if he had been hit. Through waves of pain and shock he heard words.

"There's only her and the kid."

There's only her and the kid?

As he got to his feet he felt, for the first time, real hate. Her and the kid – Louise and Karen. They were no longer men, they were mad dogs. His hands ached for a gun. It wasn't enough to lock them out, to fend them off. He wanted to smash back at them.

Working in a rage, he slammed shut the kitchen door.

"What happened, George?"

He didn't waste time in telling her.

"We need the fridge! It'll hold them."

For a moment she stood back, not understanding the new sound in his voice.

"Hurry up! They'll be through the window –"

He grabbed the fridge. It stood in a small recess outside the kitchen door, tall, white, gleaming. He tried to pull it across the stone floor. It moved a few inches and stuck.

"Push it over!"

Still not too sure, she put her hands on the smooth top. It was the one thing they'd bought themselves, the largest model in the showroom.

They were in the kitchen now, moving slowly in the darkness, not sure if he'd been shot.

George pushed her away and put his palms against the side of the fridge. He shoved. It was heavy, crammed from the vegetable keeper to the freezing compartment with food for Christmas. It rocked back towards him. He put his shoulder to it.

"Push! They're going to kill us!"

She wanted to tell him that it had cost eighty pounds, that the milk bottles would break, that –

But she put her hands to its smooth side and they both pushed and this time it went forward, end on, crashing to the stone floor. George got down to ram it against the door. What else was there? The cupboard – just inside the dining-room door.

"Hold the door," he snapped at Louise.

133

Glasses crashed together as he dragged the sideboard across the straw matting on the dining-room floor. The legs caught. Not caring that solid corners rapped his shins, he bent down and got his fingers underneath, lifting it, dragging it. When his back was against the wall he scrambled up on top of the fridge and climbed round, ramming the heavy sideboard into the space between the fridge and the wall, bruising his fingers as he clawed and shoved the heavy wood.

In the kitchen they'd found the light switch. One of them tried a shoulder against the kitchen door.

"They can't get in that way," he said to Louise. The fridge and sideboard together formed a solid wedge. "The study door! Can't we put something in there?"

He wasn't speaking to her. In his mind he had a clear map of the house. The kitchen was blocked – unless they got a sledge-hammer and battered down the top half of the door.

That left the study. And the two windows, in the dining-room and the sitting-room. Once when he'd been in his tree-house four kids from another street had tried to force their way in. He could see them now, the Schneider boy in a white T-shirt, another one they called Bricktop ... he'd jeered at them as he'd sat at the top of the rope ladder, jabbing the heels of his baseball boots into their heads. Then he'd pulled up the ladder and sat there, spitting down on them, laughing as he dodged the stones they threw up. He'd been able to command the tree-house. It had only one way in. But how could he command three different entrances?

"Christ, isn't there anything heavy?"

He'd known this before. Now he *knew*. It was in his guts, in his hands. They were fighting for their lives. He cursed himself for not using the knife on that guy when he'd had him –

The guy in the study!

"Yell out which window they're at. Stay out of sight!"

He ran through the sitting-room.

Louise got behind the wooden wall at the bottom of the stairs. They were still pounding on the kitchen door. She wanted to run away. If she dropped Karen out of the bedroom window – it wasn't very high up, they'd fall into deep snow – they could escape. Let them have Niles.

Madness was piling on madness. If they tried to touch Karen he would hit them with –

Something crossed her mind. She could *feel* herself hitting at men with something in her hands. Something in the house. What was it?

Then she remembered. She'd held it in her hands. Something that fitted into the hands as though it had been made for hitting. She ran up the stairs. There wasn't time to tell George.

With his knife stuck down inside his trousers on his left side and his left hand tied to the window post, his chest pulled across the window sill, Chris Cawsey had struggled and twisted for minutes, trying to get his right hand round to the knife. He'd had to squirm until his skin felt raw, forcing the belt to move round his stomach bringing the knife handle within reach of his fingers.

He had the blade under the flex, feeling cautiously to avoid his skin, when George came ducking into the study. He wanted this guy as a hostage. Or as a human shield. If he could drag him through the window ...

He grabbed at the knife. It jerked through the flex. He caught the wrist that held the knife. Cawsey pulled and jerked like a fox gone mad in a gin trap. It was all George could do to hold on to his wrist. This time no words were spoken. Both knew the situation had gone beyond words. To speak to a man meant you still thought of him as a fellow human being. Once you'd made up your mind that he was your enemy words became too intimate.

Cawsey tried to drag George's hands on to the woodwork, where slivers of raw glass tore at his skin. Cawsey pulled at the flex that held his other wrist until it felt as though it had cut deep into his flesh.

Cawsey shouted something – it might have been "Tom", George only cared that it was a call for help. He hit Cawsey across the face with his right hand, a swiping blow meant to shut him up. He wanted this guy in the house. When he let go to smack him Cawsey managed to jerk the knife hand free. George let go altogether to hold his forearms in front of his face. Cawsey jabbed at him with the knife.

"I'll cut your eyes out!"

George heard the words but they were only sounds. He didn't need to be told what Cawsey was trying to do. He took a step back, trying to watch where the knife was, hands ready to make another grab at the guy's wrists.

In that light it was hard to tell exactly what movements were made. Cawsey made a diagonal slash at George's hands with the knife, then he brought it down on the flex, pressing it down until he felt it sharp on the bone of his wrist. But he'd cut the flex. Too late, George saw that he was pulling himself backwards out of the window.

He went to make a grab for him but heard the others coming alone the front of the house, one of them shouting something about letting Tom Hedden have a go with the shotgun.

He moved into the wall and pressed his back against it. Christ Almighty, he could have put that guy out of action if he'd had a club or something. A big stick. A brick. Anything.

Out of the panic of events he had managed to distil an instant defensive plan, blocking the windows, using his control of the lights to put them at a disadvantage, throwing the water ... but there was a huge flaw in his reasoning. Apart from slightly scalding a couple he hadn't been able to knock any of them out. They were attackers who couldn't lose any men. He was being forced back but they were still at full strength. So far he'd been lucky, the guy with the gun hadn't thought of coming in a window himself, covering them with the gun.

They'd get around to that. Already there were signs somebody out there was using his brains. Setting the curtains on fire would have worked if they'd had the sense to set two other guys in through the windows at the same time. But they were learning, just as he was.

Outside, Norman Scutt suddenly saw how they could get into the house, all of them together. The Yank wouldn't be able to do a thing.

"Hey, Tom, you get up on the sill and go in feet first. Keep the gun pointing in, he'll never get near you."

"That's it!" one of the others exclaimed. "Blow his bloody head off."

George didn't know what to do. He could stand against the wall and make a grab for the gun barrel. No. Hedden was a farmer, a big ox of a man. In any hand-to-hand struggle he knew who would win.

Could he get the other pan of boiling water through the kitchen quickly enough to slosh it into the bastard's face? Christ, that would be too damn tricky, he might spill some over his own hand running through the three rooms. Drop the pan – and have nothing.

He could let them have the study, get back into the hall and lock the door on them. No. That old latch wouldn't hold a ten-year-old child, let alone five crazy men. There was no furniture he could drag along – in any case, that door opened inwards. He saw a film scene, a man barricading a door, hammering heavy planks across it, piling furniture – and then the door opening the other way. A comedy film.

There was only one hope. They'd have to retreat upstairs, give them the bottom of the house. Maybe he could hold them off from the landing, throw heavy stuff down on them. He thought of himself throwing chairs and beds – it would take too long. Five of them could easily rush the stairs while he was looking for stuff to throw.

It looked as though he'd have to try and jump the guy with the gun as he came through the window. Already he was being helped up on to the sill, the others getting behind him so that he could get his feet on to the ledge.

Again he saw Knapman being blown backwards in the snow. The moment he took hold of that barrel it would be his arms against the other man's.

"Louise," he called through the hall. "Lock yourself in Karen's room."

There was no answer.

He didn't blame her for running away. That was his first thought. But how? The kitchen door was blocked against an army. They'd have seen her climbing out of a window.

Unless one of them was already in the house!

He slammed the study door behind him as he dashed for the sitting-room. Whatever happened he'd make one of the bastards regret the day he was born.

CHAPTER THIRTEEN

Even as he ran he tried to think what he could use to hit the guy. It would have to be a chair, the small one at the table by the sitting-room window.

"George, I found the –"

She was coming towards him, moving so fast he thought there must be somebody behind.

"I'll get him –"

"George, it's Roger's Christmas present, don't you remember?"

"JESUS CHRIST, LOUISE, WE'RE BEING MURDERED AND YOU –"

He tried to knock whatever it was out of her hand. The sheer lunacy of Christmas presents at a time like this! She went on talking. He could have struck her to the ground.

"What're you doing? You wanted something heavy."

She shoved it in his chest, his hands feeling paper wrapped round something hard. And long. THE BASEBALL BAT!

"Louise, I –"

He didn't wait. Back into the study. Hands on the clean swell of wood. Just the right weight. Feeling for the handle. Feeling a great swell of anger and revenge coming up from his guts.

Tom Hedden had one leg dangling over the inside sill, the shotgun cradled in the crook of his right arm, finger on the triggers, his other knee pushing against wood to get through. They were shoving him from behind, shoving too hard.

George stood a few feet away. He could see the long shape of the gun barrels. He had to swing from the side, keeping out of direct line with the barrels. He had to hit the gun, knock it down. Anything else and he'd be dead – it needed a two-handed blow and to get one delivered he'd have to step away from the wall.

He waited. Let him get the other leg in. He'd have to duck to manoeuvre his head under the window spar. That was the time, when he was more or less stretched out, almost on his back. Christ, hit him now, don't wait, you'll wait too long, he'll be in, you can't time it that well. But he held on.

"We'm got you," somebody said. Hedden cursed and grunted with the effort. Then he had his left hand through, taking a grip, beginning to pull himself forward, backside sliding across the rough edges of splinters and framework. He did not care if he hurt himself, he had come to kill Henry Niles and nothing was going to stop him, neither the Yank nor Norman Scutt. He didn't care about Norman's talking, all this business about going to gaol, about killing folk. Henry Niles was the one he wanted. That's why he wouldn't let anyone else have the gun, he wanted it for Niles, to shoot him himself, like a dog worrying sheep, blow his dirty murdering heart out.

George raised the baseball bat. He shivered, though he didn't feel cold. Then he stepped away from the wall and swung the bat.

It was a good feeling. The smooth handle fitted his hands perfectly. When it hit the barrel of the shotgun there was a clean impact. The gun smacked against Tom Hedden's knees. George Magruder moved round a step, raising the bat, swinging it backhand at the man's chest, knowing he had to keep hitting him or be shot.

Tom Hedden fought to free himself from the grip of the window framework. He could see the man, the Yank, swinging the bat. He pulled the trigger.

His elbow was caught against the centre-post of the window. When the shotgun went off it was aimed at his boots.

Above the awful boom of the gun George heard the terrible scream. He knew he had not been hit. He swung the bat sideways into Tom Hedden's stomach. Raised it again, hammered it down again. Again and again.

Only when the man was limp did he make a grab for the gun. It came easily into his hands. Tom Hedden lay on his back, legs dangling into the room, head fallen backwards, face staring up at Norman Scutt and Bert Voizey and Phillip Riddaway.

They could do nothing to stop his yelling. Riddaway grabbed Tom by the shoulders, taking the weight of his backwards leaning body off his spine.

"I've got you, Tom," he said.

They dragged him headfirst, still bawling with agony, out on to the snow. Then they saw why he was making the terrifying noise. He had blown his feet off.

All four of them rushed at the window. Phil Riddaway gripped the horizontal spars, first one, then the other, cracking them away from the rest of the framework as if they were twigs. In all his life he had never seen such an awful thing. His friend, Tom Hedden! He would break the Yank's neck –

"He's got the gun!" Norman Scutt shouted, suddenly diving to the ground.

Phil didn't care. In all his life he only had two or three friends, folk who didn't laugh at him for being a big thick lump, a man who couldn't even read or write. When it hap-

139

pened to Tom it happened to him. Like a great battering ram he attacked the centre-post of the window, tearing at it with both hands, climbing knees first on to the sill, feeling it give slightly as he levered his shoulder against it, ramming his boots against the wall, knowing it was going to crack.

"I'll kill you."

"You'm dead!"

Like something out of a childish nightmare George saw the great shadow of the man coming through the window like a big black ogre.

"Die you bastard!" he yelled.

The centre-post cracked. It moved sideways. Riddaway gave a heave. It split half-way down. There was a tearing noise of splintering wood.

George held the shotgun a yard from the man's silhouette and pulled both triggers.

Both clicked. He pulled again.

The shotgun was empty. The big man came on, shoving away the stump of the centre-post. George dropped the gun and felt on the carpet for the baseball bat. His fingers found it, groped for a hold. The heavy end. Riddaway slid on to the floor. George jumped to his feet, almost tripping as he floundered backwards.

For a moment the advantage was with him, Riddaway's shape clearly outlined against the window. He swung the bat at the man's head, putting the full power of his shoulders and arms into the blow.

The bat hit Riddaway on the side of his head, just above the right ear. For a second he seemed unhurt, his hands going up to protect himself. Then he fell to the floor.

"GEORGE!"

He wanted to smash the bat down on the head, smash and smash and smash until bones broke and blood ran and brains churned to pulp.

"GEORGE! THERE'S ONE INSIDE, GEORGE!"

As he ran to answer Louise's panic-stricken yells he knew he had made a mistake in not killing the big guy. The way into the study was wide open now.

Time and time again the weight of the unconscious girl made Gregory Allsopp stumble and fall into the snow. He'd touched her face and neck and as far as his numbed fingers could tell

140

she was still warm, but her body made no movements that suggested she was still alive.

Ridiculous as it was, he was lost – blinded by snow, deafened by wind, as surely lost in two fields as he would have been on the moor. Sometimes he thought he saw lights in the village, then they were gone. A giant piston hammered inside his chest, his arms ached as though the bones were being crushed by a vice.

"HELP." He cried into the wind every few seconds. Or thought he cried into the wind. He couldn't be sure, perhaps the shouting was only in his head.

"HELP." Dando had been a village for a thousand years, a monks' settlement before that. How could all signs of man be obliterated in a few hours? Perhaps he was dreaming? He slipped again and for a moment he thought he was going to fall forward on top of the girl. No, he wasn't dreaming. He was floundering about in Soldier's Field, only a couple of hundred yards from the village, carrying a girl who might be dead or alive. Completely lost. Going round in circles. Where was Tom Hedden? What would happen tomorrow? Would there be a tomorrow? Would he and Janice be found dead in the snow? In Soldier's Field?

HELP . . . the doctor knew more about them than most, more about a wife than her husband did. Knew that Tom Hedden's wife was being worked to an early grave. Knew she could be saved for a better life. Knew there was nobody to give her a better life. Who cared about one Englishwoman who was being ground slowly but surely into the grave? The doctor knew, but the doctor was only wanted to patch her up, keep her going, relieve the pain, make her function.

HELP . . . the doctor knew but the doctor wasn't asked to tell people how to live. Only how to keep going. It should be the other way round. The doctor should say how people should live. Before they fell ill. Tell them how to organise Life. Stay alive. Enjoy Life. Instead . . . who cared about one English-woman? Not starving, not being beaten, not being deprived of her rights. Just losing her life.

HELP . . . but what did the doctor know? Really know. Tom Hedden hitting me on the head. Going out with a gun. What, *Tom Hedden*? Because of Janice? Not Tom, he didn't care that much for Janice. A burden. What did you know about people? You lived with them for years, you knew all there was

141

to know, then something happened and you found you didn't know these people at all.

HELP . . .

Gregory Allsopp's last shout was heard by two of the village men on their way back to the Inn after searching for Janice on the road which ran round the top end of Soldier's Field.

They climbed a gate into the field and walked across the slope until they found him lying on his face, his arms still clutching the girl.

"Is she all right?"

"Looks pretty far gone."

"I'll carry her to the Inn, us'll need help to carry the doctor."

"Us better get him on his feet, could die of cold lying in the snow. You go ahead with the girl. Her needs help bad."

When Gregory Allsopp came to he was being half-dragged, half-carried, his arm pulled round a man's neck. He tried to tell the man about Janice.

"Her's all right now, Doctor. Jim's got her to the Inn. You'm try to walk, Doctor."

There was something else, something he had to tell them. He couldn't remember. All he wanted to do was lie down and huddle into a ball. But the man beside him forced him to keep walking.

It was Chris Cawsey who climbed in the dining-room window. When Tom had pulled the trigger he'd slipped away from the others, knowing he could nip in another window during the commotion. He wanted to get in first, on his own. Desire burned through him. To get inside and use the knife. Maybe he hadn't taken a lot of notice of what Norman Scutt said about going to gaol, maybe he'd only been having a bit of a lark. Now he wanted to use the knife. Maybe it was the one chance he'd ever get. Use it. On something better than a sheep. Sheep were all right, for a while. But they were too easy. You didn't get anything out of it.

He was a wily one, he knew that. Norman and Tom and the others had gone at it the wrong way. He knew how to do it. Quiet like. On his own.

Being smaller than the others, he was able to climb up on the outside sill without help from behind. The table was still standing on its end where the Yank had pushed it after the fire.

142

If he kept quiet they couldn't hear him behind the table. He felt every inch of the way, hands touching lightly to feel for broken glass. The knife touched his thigh as he crouched to lift one foot, then the other, through the gap.

He was moving along the dining-room wall when Louise heard the sound.

"GEORGE!"

Chris Cawsey felt for the knife. He was well away from the window, almost in darkness. He thought of himself as a stoat, slipping through the darkness, silent, deadly. Ready to draw blood. Nobody could touch him in the dark. He liked the dark.

"Where is he?"

"The dining-room."

Chris Cawsey touched the wall with his hand. Come on, Mister Yankee fella, come and look for young Chris in the dark.

George looked into the gloom of the dining-room. He had no hope of keeping them out of the house now. Already the others would be coming through the study window. They'd have to retreat upstairs. The big guy might come round, it hadn't been too hard a bang on the head. Who was in the dining-room? It must be one man.

He leaned forward and felt for the light switch, which was just behind the doorpost. In the startled moment when the light went on, they stared at each other, George holding the bat, head just in the doorway, Cawsey with his back to the other wall, poised as if to spring, the knife in his right hand.

"Get upstairs, Louise!"

Chris Cawsey began to back towards the window, eyes darting behind him and then at George, knife held in front of his chest, pointing at George. He didn't want to fight the yank in the full light, that wasn't his idea at all.

"You dirty bastard!"

George took a two-handed grip on the baseball bat, the heavy end somewhere near his right shoulder. He saw it was the young one he'd already almost caught, the one he wanted for a hostage. Only there was no time for hostages now.

"Don't –"

As George came rushing towards him, Chris Cawsey ducked behind the table. George went on, straight at the table. He gave it a bang with the bat. Cawsey got a knee up on the window sill. George used his clenched hands to shove the table.

143

It fell towards the window, hitting Cawsey about the waist. He kicked to throw off the weight. George moved to his left, then swung the bat.

"Don't –" Cawsey yelled, raising his elbow in front of his face. The smooth curve of the bat cracked solidly into his upper arm. He let out a piercing scream. George swung the bat again, this time at his head.

"MY ARM –"

Beautiful. Bang, crack, a slight rebound. This one wasn't going to give any more trouble, this one was going to ... he stopped himself in mid-swing when he saw the blood coming through light-coloured hair. Cawsey and the table fell together, Cawsey jammed against the wall. There were ways a human body should look, lines your mind knew were right. Cawsey's position was wrong.

Two of them laid out.

One shot by his own gun.

The gun? Where was it? He'd dropped it on the floor when he'd tried to shoot the man in the window. Did they have any more shells?

He left the light on. Louise was at the top of the stairs, her face white.

"We're winning," he shouted up. "Three down, two to go."

She frowned. There was a funny expression on George's face. At the beginning – God, when was that? She looked at her watch. It was only ten to nine. It seemed to have been like this for *hours* – at the beginning he'd seemed helpless, weak and passive, looking to her for strength. Then there was a stage when he'd taken over. She'd liked that. To think that George, her bookish husband, was capable of finding ways to keep a gang of ruffians out of their house.

For the first time in years she'd felt the way she'd always wanted to feel, like a woman. Protected. Given a man to lean on. No longer leaning on herself. Even when they'd been firing the gun at the door she hadn't really felt they were in serious danger. George had been so sensible, so quick to act.

But now ... why was he looking so pleased with himself?

"What happened?" she asked. From where she stood she could see the bald spot on top of his head. Funny, some men grew their hair long to hide it, George had his cut short.

"One shot himself, I've slugged a couple with this." He held

144

up the bat, grinning. "They'll know better next time. If there is a next time."

He turned his head to listen.

"Come on, you bums."

Louise frowned to herself. She decided to go along to Karen's room. As she took a last look down the stairs she thought she heard a new noise. It didn't seem to come from down below. Then she remembered that Henry Niles was up there in the attic. It was a pity these villagers would get into serious trouble over a thing like Niles.

As she went along the corridor she heard it again. Definitely not from downstairs. Niles must be moving about in the attic. It made her shiver to think of him up there in the darkness, *that* man, evil. Ugh!

George waited at the door leading from the sitting-room, listening for the sound of them coming into the hall from the study. They'd be sure to come that way, the window was gaping open now, easy to climb in.

He heard a noise above his head. What the hell was that? Louise! She must be walking along to Karen's room. Good God, he'd forgotten all about Karen. And Niles! He smiled grimly in the semi-darkness. He hadn't done badly, not badly at all. How many handicaps could a man deal with at one time? Niles – and Karen. Five of them outside, armed. Louise trying to delude herself this wasn't serious. Be a helluva story to –

The porch light was switched on. Norman Scutt stood in the study doorway, the shotgun pointing straight at him.

"You bastard American!" Norman raised the gun. "I'll fill you with holes!"

"Yeah? With an empty gun?"

This was the bloody man who'd started it all, George was sure of it. His palm tightened on the baseball bat. Norman Scutt took a couple of steps forward.

"It ain't empty now," he said.

"Fire it then."

He braced for a jump to his left. Once he was behind the partitioning wall between the porch and the sitting-room there was no way the gun could hit him. He could stand at the corner and hit him with the bat before he could fire a shot into the sitting-room.

"AAAEEE!"

That was Louise!

"Bert's got your wife and kid then," said Norman Scutt, walking forward, holding the gun like a man who knew he had won. "Good at gettin' up drainpipes Bert is."

It had been Norman's idea, for Bert to get up on the roof of the outside porch and then swing along the front drainpipe. He'd told Bert to wait till there was some noise, then punch in a pane of glass. Bert was like a monkey when it came to getting up on roofs, trees – anything. The pipe had taken him along to the window of the fourth bedroom. He'd kicked in a pane during the noise of the fight in the dining-room.

"If he touches my –"

"You'll what, squire? You know what we'll do, we'll burn the house and the lot of you in her, you lot and that Niles friend of yours. You prefer him to the likes of we, don't you? Us be just yokels to you like, that's it, innit?"

Norman Scutt took another step towards him. George remembered a cowboy film. *Don't watch his face, watch his finger*. There was more noise upstairs, voices, banging. He began to back away. Norman Scutt came on, the shotgun held in front. George took slow backward steps, trying to remember where the furniture had been, hoping to draw Scutt into the darkness of the sitting-room.

"One sure thing, you won't get Niles," he said. "All this for nothing."

"He's still here, don't tell me any fancy tales. You'm trying to talk your way out of here then? Hard luck, Mister Yankee."

George knew he had to do something. Take the initiative. Something might startle him – he had a wild look about him, the young guy with the funny sideburns. He was well into the sitting-room now. Norman Scutt stopped.

"That'll be far enough," he said. "Just let's wait till Bert brings them down. I can see you all right, Mister Yankee."

George knew he had to move now. He had to make the right guess. Either they had some fancy plan – or the gun was empty. They'd been mad enough to kill on sight before. Why start play-acting now? Playing for time. Keep him here till the other one got at Louise and Karen. Light came into the sitting-room from two doors. He was in the middle, outlined against the dining-room door. If the gun was loaded the guy wouldn't need to aim at that range. He felt no fear. Fear belonged to the imagination. There was no need to imagine anything now.

146

It was this guy or him. Whoever could think better would win. He'd often seen himself in this situation, facing a man with a gun. Often tried to think what you could possibly do.

"Niles is dead," he said. "I killed him. He tried to take my little girl."

The tone of voice was vital. Natural. Man to man. As though the gun wasn't there.

"Oh yeh?"

"Sure! Come on, I'll show you. You won't believe how I did it. Come on, I'll show you."

He turned, deliberately casual, making no sharp movement, nothing that would scare him.

He walked towards the stairs.

"You wanted Niles, didn't you? Come on, I'll show you how I did it."

Norman Scutt followed. It had worked. Curiosity! Go off at a tangent. Keep talking.

"He's in the john, you know, the lavatory? No wonder you guys were after him! When I saw him with my little girl – d'you think they'll accuse me of murder or anything? After all, the guy was a maniac."

He said this standing on the second stair. He kept the baseball bat against his chest, hiding it from Norman Scutt. Up another three stairs. Norman Scutt advanced cautiously. He was half-convinced. The Yank wasn't acting. What did it matter anyway, there was nothing he could do. Bert and him had them cornered now. He wanted to see Niles.

George climbed each step deliberately, not looking round. He heard sounds from the other end of the upstairs corridor but he put them out of his mind. At the last step but one he turned again.

"You see this Niles? You'd never know he was a maniac, believe me. You'd never guess."

Norman Scutt moved up another two steps. George was on the landing. He stood up straight, holding the bat close to his body. He looked at the lavatory door, which Scutt couldn't see.

"God, it's awful!" he said, grimacing. Scutt moved quicker. His head was now a foot below the level of the wooden landing wall. George put his right hand to his face, as though horrified by what he could see. That was it, the moment Norman Scutt stopped concentrating on the gun and on him. He looked

147

down at his feet for the first time. George swung the baseball bat without lifting his arms, using only his wrists, bringing it round in a twirling motion, as though from the hip.

Up the bat he felt the soft impact of wood glancing against face. Then the jolting sting of wood on metal. Not just on metal. On fingers. Norman Scutt stumbled, his face caught in a gasp of surprise and pain. George put his left foot on a stair and swung the bat down, using all the force of his arms.

"You stinking bastard!" he snarled, a look of grim satisfaction on his face as he watched the other man fall backwards, first sitting, then his legs coming up, overbalancing, crashing his head against the stairs, his shoes bumping ...

George ran along the corridor. He could see the man at Karen's door, a dark solid shape.

"Come on, you slob," he shouted. "I'm not a woman."

Bert Voizey was trapped. He had his back to the door, the knife he'd been using on the latch in his right hand.

"I wasn't goin' to hurt them," he said, his voice pathetic with fear.

George was glad. The guy had a knife. He had a bat. He raised it above his head, his elbows cramped by the narrow walls. Bert Voizey tried to cower behind his elbows, dropping the knife. As the bat began to hammer down on his head and shoulders and arms he let out high-pitched roars of terror. He tried to shove past George, almost on all fours. George kneed at his face, bringing the bat down with short jabs.

He went on hitting down until there was no more movement from Voizey. When Louise opened the door he was standing above the huddled shape on the corridor floor, the bat half-raised as though to strike again.

"I got them all," he said to Louise. He was panting. "I got every stinking one of them. Come on, you pig –" he kicked Voizey's arm. Voizey didn't move. He kicked again.

"George! Stop it, you've ..."

"Have I? Have I? I'll show them, I'll –"

He swung back his right foot and drove a terrible kick into Voizey's body.

"STOP IT, GEORGE!"

He didn't listen to her. He had won. Smashed them all. The panting wouldn't stop. He'd won. He bent down and took a grip of Voizey's sleeve with his right hand, the bat still in his left. He began to drag Voizey along the corridor, pulling him, roughly, grunting, snarling things she couldn't understand.

"What is it, Mother? I'm frightened, Mother. Oh Mother, Mother –"

"It's all right, darling. They won't hurt you. Daddy's chasing them all away."

She cradled Karen in her arms, sitting on the bed as she'd done while the man had been trying to get the door open, twisted so that she covered her daughter.

At the top of the stairs George pulled and kicked at Voizey until he could shove him over the first step. He watched with a thin smile round his eyes as the unconscious man slid down till he came to rest against Scutt's legs. For a moment he stood over them with the bat, waiting for some sign of movement. There was none. He had to put down the bat to push them to the bottom of the stairs, treating them like heavy bags of coal, using his feet and his hands. When they were flat on the sitting-room floor he went back up the stairs for the bat. He patted it as he went down again, into the dining-room.

The one who'd been caught under the falling table was moving, but not much. George gave the table a kick, making the other end jab into Cawsey's chest. Cawsey moaned. *He* wouldn't be giving any trouble for a while.

He went back into the sitting-room. Now he knew the truth. All that nonsense about thresholds and civilisation. He had won! That mattered, nothing else. His chest heaved uncontrollably.

He switched on the sitting-room light. The coffee table lay on its side. Glass was strewn across the floor under the window. The house hadn't protected them, *he* had. Beaten them all. He went into the hall. The door was open. He stopped for a second. Moving cautiously, bringing the bat up, he moved towards the study.

The big fellow had gone. Run away, out of the door, run off into the snow, knowing when he was beaten. George grunted with satisfaction.

He needed to let somebody know. First he'd look outside, Christ, he'd forgotten all about Knapman – and the other guy, the one who'd shot his own feet! Pity about Knapman. Nice enough guy. As far as the other one was concerned he had probably bled to death.

He stepped out into the front porch.

149

The snow had stopped. The house was surrounded by a gleam of dazzling white. He felt tired. And proud. The greatest feeling in the world. To do it yourself. To know you could stand up to anything and anybody. To know you were a man, to be able to feel it in your guts. What a night! What a story! People would say –

The rush came from the side, out of the shadow of the porch. He swivelled to meet it, but before he could bring back the bat to swing he was hit by the bulk of Phillip Riddaway. They went over together into the snow. The weight of Riddaway collapsed on top of him. He tried to bring his knees up but they didn't have the strength to lift against that massive body. He tried to free his arms, but they were held in a bear hug.

As he struggled he felt his own feebleness under the big man's crushing weight. . . .

CHAPTER FOURTEEN

It was like drowning in a sea of heavy stone. Cushioned by snow underneath he still felt his chest and stomach being flattened by the dead weight of the man on top. He jerked and squirmed but Riddaway had him pinned down. Like a drowning man, part of him seemed totally detached. His body could feel what Riddaway was trying to do, keep his arms pinned while he levered with feet and knees to get up into a sitting position. He knew he had to hang on, not give Riddaway a chance to get up on his knees. He tried to lock his heels round Riddaway's ankles, to keep Riddaway's legs straightened out. Riddaway's forehead butted sideways into his face. He tried to bite Riddaway's ear. As a boy he'd wrestled like this, scrambling fights with boys, rolling over and over on sandlots and grass parks and asphalt play areas. Like a smell that can suddenly evoke haunting pictures from a forgotten past, the feel of another body on top of his own, pressed hard from head to foot, brought out long-dead emotions and memories. He jammed the side of his head against Riddaway's face, knowing that only by sticking tight could he stop Riddaway butting him senseless. Bracing his right knee he tried to jerk his body

150

up, trying to turn Riddaway over on his side. There was no lifting that weight. He saw the white wall of the house, the darkness of the sky, the light above the porch, a window, objects flashing meaninglessly across his eyes as scenery whirls before the screaming face on the roller-coaster. They were locked in a pulverising intimacy, total strangers who understood only that the other was, like himself, fighting for life. To live the other had to be destroyed.

He forced his temple against Riddaway's cheek, slowly manoeuvring his head so that he could sink his teeth into some soft part of the other man's face. Riddaway drew his head back for another butt, but he craned his neck to keep their heads pressed together. Under his body Riddaway's right hand felt for a hold on his wrist. There was a slight easing of the bear hug. He jerked his body in an upwards arch, desperately pulling his arms up out of Riddaway's powerful grip. Riddaway brought up his right knee, jabbing into his groin. He drew up his left knee, fencing with the big man's leg, smothering his movements. He was no match for the brute power that held him to the ground. He smelled liquor. And sweat. Old, stale, rancid sweat. How could people live like that? Was this a man – like himself? Did they really speak the same language?

For a moment he thought of stopping his struggles and speaking to this man. A reasonable tone of voice. Say, pal, what the hell are we doing this *for*?

He felt his nose and chin press into skin. He pulled his lower jaw down until he could feel his teeth touching soft flesh.

There was a mad, insensate, electrifying, hysterical, sadistic glee about it. Biting into flesh. Bite, bite, bite! Glee and hatred and revenge and power. Riddaway's body jolted into brutal jerks, the great fish electrocuted by the searing pain of the barb. Big hands tore themselves free from the weight of the two bodies and beat at his head. His own arms were free then. Four hands grappled and pulled and strained at each other. There was a terrible strength in his jaw. He wanted to sink in, deeper and deeper, to destroy.

Riddaway began to roar. His palms splayed across George's forehead and cheek, fingers digging for soft spots, George's hands groping for Riddaway's ears, his hair, his jaw quivering with an awful tension, teeth clamping tighter and tighter on a wad of flesh. He had to hang on. Riddaway's hands would tear

151

him in pieces. Riddaway's thumbs jabbed into his eyes. He screwed his eyelids tight, tighter. He screwed Riddaway's ears in his fists.

Riddaway punched him. He bit harder. Riddaway tore at his hair. There was no pain. He could feel it, but there was no pain. Riddaway plucked at his throat, thumb hooking round his windpipe. Riddaway drew up his knees, forcing his back into the air, trying to bring his knee down into his stomach. He let himself be pulled by Riddaway, hanging on like a terrier with its teeth into the soft belly of a dog twice its size. Riddaway got a grip on his throat with both thumbs and began to squeeze.

He jerked his knee up into Riddaway's groin. He felt the quivering tension of his jaws, biting through flesh, teeth trying to meet teeth, muscles of iron under the chin. He gouged harder on Riddaway's ears. One hand left his throat, crushing fingers wrapped round his wrist and tore his hand away from the ear. He jerked his knee up again, feeling it ram home.

Riddaway's fist crashed into his eye. He bit harder. He could never let go. His eyes were shut, lids squeezed so tight there was a singing in his ears. Riddaway got a knee on to his stomach.

His guts! He jerked sideways. They fell over. He let himself be pulled by his teeth, bringing the heel of his palm up to Riddaway's nose.

When he felt himself free of the weight he opened his jaws. Riddaway's hands stopped tearing at his face. He threshed like a salmon, pushing himself away, getting to his knees. Riddaway had both hands on his face, still bawling with unspeakable pain.

George was running before he got off his hands and knees, knowing only that he had to get out of the reach of Riddaway's hands. He ran for the front door.

Louise, he shouted, but there was no life in his jaw.

Riddaway was coming behind him. He didn't have to look round. He *knew*. They were like one being, existing only in their lust to kill the other.

He forced his leaden legs to move, palming himself off the walls, breasting through the door.

Louise! He did not hear his own shout, did not know if it left his mouth. Run, run from the man behind, run. Across the sitting-room, shins brushing aside some piece of furniture,

152

feeling the hatred of Riddaway coming behind him, feeling the big hands reaching out.

Louise was there, on the stairs.

She had the shotgun, holding it in both hands. Two men lay at the bottom of the stairs, one looking at him. He felt his feet scrabbling over the uneven lumps of their bodies. The gun! Louise would not move. The gun!

He had his palms on the stairs, crawling, pulling. The gun! He had no strength. It was a dream. His muscles were dead. He forced himself up, his hands on the same step as her shoes. A dream where he spoke but no words came from his lips.

Then he was falling. Louise's face looking down at his. Louise not moving. Louise holding the gun. Not falling, being pulled. Hands on his ankles. His fingers tearing at carpet, digging for a hold, his feet kicking against the hands. Louise not moving.

He got his fingers under the edge of the stair carpet. Hold on. Looking round. Riddaway's face, red, wet. Carpet being dragged through his burning fingers. Feeling the iron grip on his ankles. Looking up at Louise.

Help me!

Louise did not move until she saw the big man pull George to his knees, dragging him away from the stairs. He dragged him as if George was a wild dog he had by the ears and was holding at arm's length. The big man's face was wet with blood, a thick smear of shiny redness that made her feel faint. George must have done that to the big man, no wonder he was kicking at George, holding him by the shoulders of his sweater, George on one knee, the other foot scrabbling for a grip on the floor, the big man bent forward, his boot making dull thudding noises as it toed into George's legs and stomach.

"Help me!"

How could she help George! There was nothing she could do to that big man. They were like lions fighting in a dark cage, the sitting-room coffee table going over, two figures tied together in a pulverising, lurching, hurtling, kicking whirlpool of crashing furniture, guttural noises....

He punched at Riddaway, but his fists made no impression. He kicked Riddaway's legs, but his shoes seemed to bounce. Riddaway held him by the shoulders, not letting him close enough for another bite. He felt the heavy toecap jarring on

153

his shin. Riddaway spun him round, trying to throw him to the floor. Louise had just looked at him. Riddaway stamped down on his feet. He knew what was happening, as though he had done this many times before, even in the dark he knew. His legs were weary, but he made them move. Riddaway's heel cracked down on his toes. He felt the crunch, but no pain. Louise had the gun, but she hadn't moved to help. It was all he could think of, Louise not moving, then he stopped even thinking about that. Riddaway was trying to throw him to the floor, then stomp him. Don't go down. Hold on. He got his fingers at Riddaway's face, jabbing and tearing at skin. Riddaway kicked at his ankle from the side, trying to boot away his feet. He half fell, but held on to Riddaway, his face, his clothes, he didn't know what he was holding. He punched at Riddaway's face, but there was no real impact. The great hands were forcing him down, swinging him round.

They were at the door into the hall. For a moment Riddaway's face was in the light. He tried to slip downwards out of his sweater, twisting convulsively. Riddaway grabbed his hair.

Two fingers appeared in front of his face. He could see them clearly, index and second, jutting out, other fingers bent back to the palm. He watched the two fingers jab at Riddaway's eyes. He felt them sink into something soft. They were his fingers. He jabbed again. He could see it clearly, pink skin against red blood.

"GAAAAHH!"

Riddaway stumbled back, clapping his hands to his eyes.

"AAAAAHHH."

George couldn't feel his legs. But they moved. He moved, without knowing why. He was in the hall, then in the outside porch. He knew nothing except that he was out in the snow. There it was. The bat. He had to pick it up. It came up off the ground but he couldn't feel it in his hands. He had to go back inside. He had to kill the big man. He had to ...

Riddaway's head was forward, almost on his chest, his hands flat over his eyes, swaying, inhuman bellowing, a wounded animal to be pulped into the ground before it could kill. He hit the animal once, then twice. His arms moved slowly. The animal tried to run, but the animal was blinded, it banged into the wall. He hit the animal wherever was nearest, on its back, head, arms. It had to be destroyed. The animal tried to get up, its hands trying to catch the bat. He swung down at his hands,

154

knocking them away. The animal couldn't see, its eyes were half-shut. He hit the animal on the forehead.

Louise was beside him. Holding his arm. Saying something. Didn't she realise the animal had to be destroyed, once and for all, smashed into the ground, destroyed?

Then he couldn't swing the bat any more.

"Kill it, kill it," he kept mumbling as the men surrounded him and pinned his arms and pulled him away. "Kill it, kill it."

Sergeant Wills looked round the sitting-room.

"Jesus Christ," he said. "Jesus Christ!"

CHAPTER FIFTEEN

It took half a day to get a snowplough along the narrow road from Compton Wakley to Dando and then up to Trencher's Farm, a plough followed by a mechanical digger which scooped up snow and dropped it on the other side of the high banks and hedging.

About half-past eight on Christmas Eve George phoned the Venner farm to tell Louise, who had gone there with Karen, that he was being brought home by car from the county hospital.

"They say I'm okay," he said. His voice sounded deeper.

"That's good," she said. "We could stay here with Mr. and Mrs. Venner – for tonight? I mean, do you think we should go back to . . . it'll be very cold, all those windows broken. . . ."

"I don't suppose you really want to go back there at all, do you? I'll come to the Venner's. Are you – all right? You and Karen? I guess it was pretty awful. . . ."

"Whatever you think."

"I'll see you at the Venner's. 'Bye. . . ."

" 'Bye."

He put down the phone, wishing he had said 'I love you'.

They left the hospital by a side entrance used for delivering foodstuffs. He walked along a ramp on which were stacked bright metal bins full of waste. He walked stiffly, almost every part of him burning slowly. The young doctor and the orderly

155

offered to help him but he walked unaided. The orderly kept saying he'd never seen so many reporters and television blokes.

George wasn't too sure from what the doctors and nurses had said whether they regarded him as a hero or a villain. It didn't seem too important, either way. The car left the hospital unnoticed.

His eyes fixed on the piled snow and white banks caught in the beam of the car headlights, he tried to sum it up in his own mind, but he seemed to be numbed, in a vacuum, as though he didn't know who he was any more. He could see pictures of himself, but it was impossible to associate himself with the man who had done those things. It was as if he'd been catapulted from a seat in the movies into the movie itself. It wasn't real. Since this morning, when they'd brought him to the hospital, things had become real again. Already he was thinking of it – all of it – not as something that had actually happened to him but as something made real only by the words of the people he'd spoken to. The policeman, an English policeman with a thick accent, sitting by the bed, asking him questions, telling him the answers to his own questions.

"We'll be making charges. It won't be your responsibility. You'll be a witness. I don't know what the charges will be, not yet awhile. Difficult case, manslaughter – or attempted murder. They're giving the Hedden man blood transfusions now. Shot all his toes off! Cawsey, he's got a fractured skull for sure. Hit him proper, you did, had a real go, didn't you?"

He didn't understand why the policeman seemed to find this 'having a go' slightly amusing. Bill Knapman was dead. Cawsey, Voizey, Scutt and Riddaway were being X-rayed. They'd be taken to prison once they'd been patched up. Cawsey, Voizey, Scutt and Riddaway. He could even say their names in a local accent. He repeated them over and over again in his mind. Like a line of poetry, an old ballad maybe. Their names would become famous. Four men heading for gaol. Hedden as well.

And Henry Niles. Taken back to the insane place. Not a scratch on him, crying like a baby when they opened the attic door, crying because he didn't like the dark. Probably never understand what had happened.

And the others. Gregory Allsopp, suffering from slight exposure. Janice Hedden, severe exposure. The policeman said they couldn't get anything out of her. Nobody had touched

156

her. She must have run across the field making for home and lost her way. She would be all right. She would go back to her mother and brothers. What would happen to the Heddens now, with Tom Hedden a cripple facing jail? What would happen to the Knapmans?

He didn't even know if Cawsey, Voizey, Scutt and Riddaway had wives and children. He knew nothing about them, except that they had come to his house to kill him. The policeman more or less said they were bad characters, but policemen always did.

WHY?

Was it his fault? Would these men have come in a mob if Niles had been in the house of another villager, somebody they knew? Would they really have killed Niles?

He winced as the car took a sharp corner and he slid an inch or two along the seat. Was it his fault? A terrible event had taken place, lives lost and ruined. Why? He had come as a total stranger, into a life and place he didn't even begin to understand. If he hadn't come, looking for peace to write a book, would Knapman still be alive? Would Hedden be a cripple? Would Cawsey, Voizey, Scutt and Riddaway be facing gaol?

He'd come to write a book about Branksheer, a nice bit of recherché academicism, an amusing dabble into the jolly, bawdy, boisterous England of the past. These men were English – yet they would never have heard of Branksheer.

There was a darker, deeper question. One he tried not to allow shape to, something lurking in the shapeless mass of words and images that danced and seethed at the back of his mind. . . .

It was not until they'd got Karen to sleep and until the Venners had finally gone to bed that he and Louise were alone. It was a small, farmhouse bedroom, cold despite a two-barred electric fire, its only light a naked bulb in the middle of the low ceiling.

"Well?" he said.

They stood on either side of the lumpy bed, postponing the return to homely routine that undressing would mean. Her voice was thin and apologetic. She didn't look at him.

"I'm sorry."

"What do you mean?"

"I behaved very badly. I didn't do anything. . . ."

157

"*You* didn't behave badly. I –"

Could she answer the question? He realised that he was frightened to ask her.

"I wasn't any help to you. I'm sorry, I lost my head. I couldn't believe it was really happening, when you –"

"Don't talk about it. I should have –"

"No. I was being a bitch. I don't know what was getting into me."

It began to dawn on him that she was talking about something else. He stared at her, his face puzzled. Her fingers played nervously with the comb that held her Jane Austen bun.

"It never meant anything, honestly. It was all stupid. It was just a way of getting back at you ... you were always in the right, Patrick just seemed like a –"

"Patrick! Patrick! Ryman? What the hell has he got to do with –"

Then he laughed noiselessly, shaking his head in bewilderment, although he knew he was only acting, because he knew exactly what she meant.

"You mean, all that stuff last night, murderers and guns and – all that and you're thinking about Ryman?"

"It was all I could think of," she said, turning her face away. The comb came out of her bun. Her dark hair fell in a pony tail over her curved back. "I don't deserve you, George, it's true, I don't, I don't ..." she began to sob.

"You funny woman," he said.

He went round the bed and put his arms round her head, comforting her. It happened to both of them at the same time. The stiffness made it seem even more vital. They made love on top of the bedcover, neither noticing the cold. It was the first time in his life that he was able to make love to a woman with the light on.

He didn't have room in his head for *thoughts*. He had won. The man who had won. The man who *knew*.

It was during breakfast in the Venner kitchen that she remembered Jeremy and Sophia. They put through a call to Sophia's London number. There was no answer. Charlie Venner said he would drive them down to Trencher's. When they saw that there was no sign of Jeremy's car at the house they sat in Charlie Venner's Land-Rover at the end of the road, not

158

saying much, the sight of the house making them think of the night before. George told himself that he and Louise were happier together at this moment than they'd been for years.

"We could leave a note on the gatepost," said Charlie Venner.

But after about twenty minutes Jeremy's Vauxhall estate wagon came up the road from Dando Monachorum. They got out of the Land-Rover.

Jeremy faced them aggressively, a tweed cap low over his face.

"I say, what the Dickens has been going on?" he demanded. "We were trying to phone you all yesterday. We got stuck in a drift, had to be dug out, we had to stay the night in a simply dreadful pub."

"The snow put our phone out of order," Louise said.

"Bloody hell, it's *too* bad."

"We had a spot of bother, too, old man," said George, holding Louise's hand. "We –"

"Bother? Do you think we were having a bloody picnic? At least you were nice and snug in your own house. *We* had a ghastly time!"

They both began to laugh.

Only Karen kept a straight face. She was distantly polite when her three cousins got out of the estate wagon. She didn't speak until they were heading back up the road to the Venner place.

"Mummy?"

"Yes, darling?"

"Will those nasty men be sent to gaol for killing our pussy cat?"

George looked at Louise. Their eyes met above Karen's head. It was only one of the questions they never wanted to have to answer.

A NOTE ON THE AUTHOR

Gordon Williams was born in Paisley and is the author of over twenty books, of which *From Scenes Like These* was shortlisted for the first ever Booker Prize. He has also written extensively for television, has worked as a journalist and as the commercial manager of Chelsea FC.